The Three Investigators in

The Mystery of the
Whispering Mummy

ALFRED HITCHCOCK

and **The Three Investigators** in

The Mystery
of the
Whispering
Mummy

Text by Robert Arthur

Illustrated by Harry Kane

RANDOM HOUSE · NEW YORK

This title was originally cataloged by the Library of Congress as follows:
Arthur, Robert.
Alfred Hitchcock and the Three Investigators in the mystery of the whispering
mummy.   Illustrated by Harry Kane.   New York, Random House [1965]
185 p.   Illus.   22 cm.   (Alfred Hitchcock mystery series, 3)
I. Title   (Series)
PZ7.A744Aj   65 — 17278
ISBN: 0-394-81220-4   ISBN: 0-394-91220-9 (lib. ed.)

Contents

For Latecomers Only: INTRODUCTION
by Alfred Hitchcock   1

1   AN EXCITING LETTER   3
2   THE MUMMY WHISPERS   14
3   JUPITER TRIES MIND READING   25
4   THE CURSE OF THE MUMMY   33
5   SUDDEN DANGER   40
6   A SURPRISING VISITOR   55
7   THE JACKAL GOD APPEARS   67
8   TRAPPED!   75
9   STARTLING DISCOVERIES   90
10 NO ESCAPE FOR THE PRISONERS   101
11 BOB AND JUPITER ARE WORRIED   110
12 A WILD FLIGHT   117
13 JUPITER HAS SUSPICIONS   127
14 TOO MANY QUESTION MARKS   144
15 JUPITER IS ON HIS OWN   153
16 CAPTIVE AND CAPTOR   161
17 AMAZING REVELATIONS   170
18 MR. HITCHCOCK ASKS SOME QUESTIONS   178

For Latecomers Only: Introduction by Alfred Hitchcock

The following words are solely for the benefit of those of you who have come in late. If you are already familiar with The Three Investigators, you may skip this brief commercial and proceed directly to the entertainment portion of the program. Fortunately, this is a book so you can accomplish this matter merely by turning a page or two. If this were television, you would have to sit through the whole thing.

To fill you in on what has happened in the past, The Three Investigators is a firm of youthful detectives formed by three enterprising lads: Jupiter Jones, Pete Crenshaw, and Bob Andrews.

Jupiter, by his own admission, is the brains of the outfit. Bob takes notes on all cases and does research. Pete, strong and agile, is invaluable as Jupiter's assistant on active missions.

The boys live in Rocky Beach, a small city on the shore of the Pacific Ocean some miles from Hollywood. Here in Southern California, distances are so great that an automobile is a vital necessity. None of the boys is quite old enough to drive, but their car problem was solved when Jupiter won the use of an automobile, complete with chauffeur, in a contest. The car, a gold-plated Rolls Royce, is theirs for thirty days only, and they are putting it to good use.

Headquarters for The Three Investigators is a converted mobile home trailer situated in The Jones Salvage Yard, which is run by Jupiter's uncle and aunt, Titus and Mathilda Jones. The trailer has a small office in it, a lab, a dark room, and equipment which the boys rebuilt from junk that came into the salvage yard. It can be entered by certain secret passages that only youthful individuals can negotiate.

You now know all you need to be on your own. I deplore the modern trend toward coddling youth. Therefore you are now urged to read the book for yourself to learn the remainder.

Alfred Hitchcock

Chapter 1

An Exciting Letter

"SAVE ME! Save me!" cried a strange, high-pitched voice in great terror. "Please save me!"

The Three Investigators—Jupiter Jones, Pete Crenshaw, and Bob Andrews—heard the cry but ignored it and continued working. The speaker was their mascot, the trained mynah bird, Blackbeard, whom they had acquired in a previous case. It picked up words and phrases with astounding ease and delighted in trying them out.

"Jupiter!" Mrs. Mathilda Jones, Jupiter's aunt, glanced at Blackbeard's cage which was hung from a length of board inside The Jones Salvage Yard. "You've been letting that bird watch too much television. It's talking like somebody in one of those mystery programs."

"Yes, Aunt Mathilda," Jupiter said. He puffed as he picked up an old front door. "Where shall I put this?"

"With the other doors," his aunt told him. "You boys! Stop lounging around! We have a lot of work to do and time is going fast."

Time wasn't going fast enough to suit The Three Investigators. Under Mrs. Mathilda Jones' direction, they were engaged in an investigation they would have preferred to skip—they were investigating how much work three boys could do on a hot day. Mrs. Jones, a large woman, really ran The Jones Salvage Yard. Jupiter's Uncle Titus merely did the buying for it and was away on buying trips most of the time. This was a day when Aunt Mathilda was having one of her frequent clean-up impulses. When that happened, Jupiter and any of his friends who might be handy were pressed into service.

As the three boys worked, moving batches of building material and generally tidying things up, they itched to get back into Headquarters—their hidden mobile home trailer—and to work on some new mystery. Their recent successes had given them confidence in their ability as investigators—perhaps too much confidence.

But no relief came their way until the postman turned into the main gate, driving his small three-wheeled vehicle. He dropped a bundle of letters into the antique iron mail basket which was screwed to the front of the salvage yard office and went on his way.

"Mercy!" Mathilda Jones exclaimed. "I forgot all about the registered letter your Uncle Titus wanted mailed, Jupiter."

She fished into a capacious pocket and brought out a slightly rumpled envelope. She smoothed out the wrinkles and handed the letter to Jupiter.

"Ride down to the post office right away and register it, Jupiter," she said. "Here's some money. Try to get it into the morning mail."

"I'll get it there, Aunt Mathilda," the stocky boy promised. "Pete and Bob will take over for me while I'm gone. They've been complaining that what they need is a good workout."

While Bob and Pete spluttered with indignation, Jupiter hopped on his bike and shot through the gate toward town. Mrs. Jones chuckled.

"All right, boys," she said, "I'll give you the rest of the morning off. You can have a meeting or build something or do whatever it is you do back there behind all that junk."

She gestured toward the various piles of salvage material which artfully concealed Jupiter's outdoor workshop and—although she did not realize it—Headquarters. Then she started for the office.

"I'd better look over the mail right now," she said. "There might be something for Jupiter in it. He's been sending away for samples of a lot of awfully strange things lately."

Glad to be finished with the heavy work, the boys followed her. Mrs. Jones scooped up the mail and began to leaf through it.

"A card from an auction house," she said. "A bill. A check for that old steam boiler. Hmmm." She tucked a letter under her arm and went on. "Another bill. A post card from my sister Susan. An advertisement to come live in Florida." That made her chuckle again. Then she looked at another letter, said "Hmmm" once more, and tucked that under her arm, too.

She went on with the mail. There were a couple of letters for Titus Jones, probably inquiries about special articles. The Jones Salvage Yard was widely known as the place to go when you needed something that was odd, unusual, or hard to find. Among other things, Titus Jones had an old pipe organ for sale. Sometimes, in the evening, he would go into the yard and play "Asleep in the Deep" on it. Hans and Konrad, the big Bavarian brothers who did the heavy work and drove the Joneses' two trucks, would gather around him and sing the words in a very melancholy manner.

When she had finished looking over the mail, Mrs. Jones shook her head.

"No," she said, "nothing for Jupiter."

She turned to go into the office, then turned back. By the twinkle in her eyes the boys could see she was teasing them.

"However," she said, "there are two letters here addressed to The Three Investigators. That's your new club, isn't it?"

Some time before, when they were all interested in solving puzzles and contests, the boys had formed a puzzle club. It was because of this interest, in fact, that Jupiter had entered a contest sponsored by the local Rent-'n-Ride Auto Rental Company and had won the use of an antique Rolls Royce, complete with chauffeur, for thirty days.

Having a car available, the boys had immediately set up the firm of The Three Investigators to tackle any real-life puzzles that they could find. However, Mrs. Jones, who was a little absent-minded about anything not connected with her business, still thought of their enterprise as a club. No amount of explaining could shake the notion from her head, so the boys ceased to try.

Now, with restrained excitement, Pete took the letters she handed him. Mrs. Jones went into the salvage yard office. The two boys made a beeline for Headquarters.

"We won't even look to see who they're from until we get into Headquarters," Pete said. "This may be official business."

"Right," Bob agreed. "Now I can start our correspondence file. It's all set up, but up to now we haven't had any mail."

They threaded their way between piles of junk until they came to Jupiter's workshop. It was equipped with a drill press, a lathe, a band saw, a small printing press, and other useful items. All these things had come into the yard as junk and Jupiter and the others had put them back into working condition.

A high board fence surrounded the yard, and a roof six feet wide on the inner side not only protected the better merchandise but also protected the workshop.

There were large plastic covers to be used during the brief rainy seasons.

A large section of corrugated pipe—the kind used for culverts—seemed to block passage behind the workshop. However, when the boys moved a piece of old iron grating that was hidden by the printing press, the mouth of the pipe was uncovered. The boys crawled into it. They replaced the grating, then, on hands and knees, went forward about forty feet. The pipe, after disappearing partly underground and partly beneath some useless-looking iron beams, opened at the other end, directly under the concealed mobile home trailer which the boys had converted into Headquarters. When Mr. Jones found he couldn't sell the old trailer, he had told Jupiter and his friends that they could use it.

A trap door opened upward. They scrambled through this and were inside, in a tiny office fitted up with a desk that had been damaged in a fire, several chairs, a typewriter, a filing cabinet, and a telephone. On the desk there was an old-fashioned table radio. Jupiter had connected a microphone to its loudspeaker that enabled the boys to listen to any phone conversation together. The remainder of the trailer had been converted into a tiny darkroom, a miniature lab, and a washroom.

Because it was dark inside—the trailer was surrounded by piles of junk outside—Pete switched on the light that hung over the desk. Then the boys plopped themselves down and stared at the letters.

"Hey!" Pete yelped with excitement. "This one comes from the office of Alfred Hitchcock! Let's open it first!"

Bob looked excited. Alfred Hitchcock writing to them? It had to be about a case, because Mr. Hitchcock had promised them that if any mystery came to his attention, that seemed to need their talents, he would let them know.

"Let's save that for last," he said. "It's probably the most interesting one. Anyway, don't you think we should wait for Jupe before we open these?"

"After the way he tried to pull a fast one on us just now?" Pete said indignantly. "And tried to get Mrs. Jones to work us to a frazzle? Besides, you're in charge of records and research and that certainly includes mail, doesn't it?"

The argument was good enough for Bob. He began to slit open the less important letter. But as he did so, he noted several things about the envelope and an idea occurred to him.

"Before we read this letter," he said, "let's see if we can deduce anything from it. Jupe said we should practice deduction whenever we had a chance."

"What can you tell from a letter without even reading it?" Pete demanded skeptically. But Bob was already studying the envelope, both back and front. It was light lilac. He smelled it; it had a lilac scent. Then he glanced at the folded sheet of paper inside. It, too, looked and smelled like lilac. At the top of the note-paper was an engraved picture of two playful kittens.

"Mmm," Bob said, and put his fingers to his fore-head as if thinking deeply. "Yes, it's coming to me. The writer of this letter is a lady of—oh, about fifty, I guess. She is little and plump, and dyes her hair, and probably talks a lot. Also, she's crazy about cats. She's good-hearted but a little careless sometimes. Usually she's cheerful but when she wrote this letter she was feeling very upset about something."

Pete's eyes popped.

"Gleeps!" he said. "You can deduce all that from the envelope and the paper, without even reading the letter?"

"Sure." Bob was nonchalant about it. "I forgot to add that she also has a good deal of money and is probably active in charity work."

Pete took the envelope and the letter and examined them, scowling. But presently a look of understanding crossed his face.

"Those kittens on her letterhead tell us she probably like cats," he said. "The fact that she put the post-age stamp on slantwise and tore it a little getting it out of the stampbook, indicates that she's a little care-less. Her letter starts with the lines slanting upward across the page, which is often the sign of a cheerful person. At the end of the letter, though, the lines be-gin to slant downward, showing she was getting very upset and unhappy about something."

"That's it," Bob said. "Deduction is simple when you put your mind to it."

"And when you have Jupe to give you some lessons," Pete added. "But what I want to know is how you can tell her age and size and that she talks a lot and has money and is active in charity and dyes her hair. You'd have to be Sherlock Holmes to be able to tell all that."

"Well," Bob told him, grinning, "the return address is in a part of Santa Monica where the houses are very expensive. Women who live there are usually rich, and they are active in charity because, my mother says, they don't have enough housework to do to keep themselves busy."

"Okay," Pete challenged him. "Now what about her age and size and the fact that she talks too much and dyes her hair?"

"Well," Bob answered, "she uses lilac-colored paper with a lilac scent and green ink. It's mostly older women who go in for that sort of thing. But to be honest with you, I have an Aunt Hilda who uses exactly that kind of paper. She's fifty and small and talkative and dyes her hair, so I figure this"—he studied the paper to get the name on the signature—"this Mrs. Banfry is probably the same kind of person."

Pete laughed.

"You did a good job even if you did throw that last part in as a guess," he said. "Now let's see what she says." He scanned the letter.

" 'Dear Three Investigators,' " Pete began reading. " 'My very dear friend, Miss Waggoner, in Hollywood, has told me how you found her missing parrot, Little Bo-Peep——' "

At this point Bob nimbly pulled the paper from between Pete's fingers. Obviously Mrs. Banfry had heard about their previous exciting case *The Mystery of the Stuttering Parrot.*

"I'm in charge of records," Bob reminded Pete. Having a brace on his leg from a fall on a local hill when he was small, Bob was slightly handicapped in the more active exploits of the team. Accordingly, his job was to keep all the records, do research, and make full notes on all the cases.

"Letters," Bob added, "are in my department, at least when Jupe isn't here. So I'll read this one."

Pete muttered, but gave in. Bob settled back and read the handwritten letter swiftly. The facts were very simple. Mrs. Banfry had an Abyssinian cat, named Sphinx, that she treasured greatly. Sphinx had been missing for a week. The police couldn't find the cat, and Mrs. Banfry had put ads in the local papers without results. Now, would The Three Investigators, who had done such a fine job finding the parrot for her friend, Miss Waggoner, be good enough to help find her darling cat? She would be truly obliged. It was signed, "Yours most sincerely, Mrs. Mildred Banfry."

"A missing cat," Pete said thoughtfully. "Well, it's a case, anyhow. Sounds like a nice, quiet case, easy on the nerves. I'll give her a ring and say we'll take it."

"Wait." Bob stopped him as he reached for the telephone. "Let's see what Mr. Hitchcock has to say."

"That's right," Pete agreed. Bob was already slitting open the long envelope. He drew out a sheet of expensive-looking bond stationery, which had the name of Alfred Hitchcock engraved at the top, and started to read it aloud.

However, after the first sentence he stopped reading aloud and his eyes raced on, devouring the facts contained in the letter. When he had finished, he looked at Pete with wide eyes.

"Wow!" he said. "Read it. You'll never believe it if I tell you. You'll say I'm making it up."

Curiously, Pete took the letter and started to read. When he had finished, he looked across at Bob, goggle-eyed.

"Gleeps!" he whispered. And then he asked a question that anyone who had not read the letter would have thought a rather unusual one. "How can a 3,000-year-old mummy whisper?" he asked.

Chapter 2

The Mummy Whispers

BEHIND THE FACTS contained in the letter that Alfred Hitchcock had written lay certain events of a more peculiar and eerie quality than anything in which The Three Investigators had previously been involved.

Some ten or twelve miles from Rocky Beach and The Jones Salvage Yard, a small canyon pierced the hills outside Hollywood. It was a canyon on whose steep sides were nestled a few large and expensive homes, surrounded by trees and bushes. One of these was an old, Spanish-style mansion, one wing of which had been turned into a private museum by the owner, Professor Robert Yarborough, a noted Egyptologist.

A row of tall French windows reaching down to the floor faced a tiled terrace. The windows were closed, making the room oddly hot and oppressive in the late afternoon sunshine. Near the windows stood several statues that had been taken from old tombs in Egypt. One statue, made of wood, was a representation of the ancient Egyptian god, Annubis. It had a human body with the head of a jackal. The shadow of the jackal head fell across the floor, forming a dark, inky blot of a rather unnerving shape.

Other relics taken from the tombs of ancient Egypt crowded the room. Metal masks that seemed to smile with secret knowledge hung on the walls. Clay tablets, gold jewelry, and ancient scarabs—images of sacred beetles, carved from green jade by workmen long-dead —brooded in glass cases.

In an open space near the windows stood a wooden mummy case with a lid on which was carved the features of the mummy inside. It was a very plain mummy case with no gold leaf or painted colors to make it look rich and luxurious. It was, however, a mummy case that held a mystery. It was the pride of Professor Robert Yarborough, a small, somewhat plump man with a dignified-looking goatee and gold-rimmed spectacles.

When he was younger, Professor Yarborough had headed many expeditions to Egypt. On these expeditions he had discovered lost tombs carved into rocky hillsides, holding the mummies of long-dead pharaohs and their wives and servants, together with jewels and other objects. He kept the relics in his museum, where he was writing a book about his discoveries.

The mummy case and the mummy inside it had arrived just a week earlier. Professor Yarborough had discovered this mummy fully twenty-five years before. But since he was busy at that time, working on a long and difficult assignment, he had loaned the mummy to a museum in Cairo, Egypt. When he retired, he had asked the Egyptian government to send the mummy to him for further study. Now that he had time, he wanted to see if he could unravel the mystery which surrounded it.

On this particular afternoon, two days before the boys had received Alfred Hitchcock's letter, Professor Yarborough was standing in the museum room, nervously tapping a pencil against the lid of the mummy case—a lid that could be lifted off like the lid of a chest. Indeed, the mummy case was really nothing but a special wooden chest in which the mummy rested.

With the professor was Wilkins, his butler, a tall, thin man who had worked for him for years.

"Are you sure you want to do this, sir, after the shock you had yesterday?" Wilkins asked.

"I must see if it happens again, Wilkins," Professor Yarborough said firmly. "First, please open the windows. I hate a closed room."

"Yes, sir." Wilkins swung open the nearest French windows. Many years before, Professor Yarborough had been caught in a closed tomb for two days, and since then he had had a strong aversion to being in a closed room of any kind.

When the windows were opened, Wilkins lifted off the lid of the mummy case and leaned it against the case. Both men bent to peer in.

Some people might not enjoy looking at a mummy,

although there is nothing offensive about one. Soaked in bitumen and other substances to preserve them, then carefully wrapped in linen, the bodies of dead kings and nobles of ancient Egypt were preserved almost intact through the centuries. It was part of the religious belief of the time that they must be so preserved for their proper entrance into the next world. For this same reason many clothes, ornaments, tools, and jewels that they owned in life were buried with them—to be used in the world to come.

The mummy inside bore the name Ra-Orkon. The linen cocoon in which it was wrapped had been partly opened so that the professor could see Ra-Orkon's face. It was an elderly, sensitive face, that looked as if it were carved from some dark wood. The lips were slightly parted, as if it were about to speak. The eyes were shut.

"Ra-Orkon looks very peaceful, sir," Wilkins commented. "I do not think he will speak to you today."

"I hope not." Professor Yarborough set his lips. "It is not natural, Wilkins, for a mummy dead for three thousand years to talk. Even to whisper. It is not natural at all."

"Very unnatural, sir," the butler agreed.

"Yet he did whisper to me yesterday," the professor said. "When I was alone in the room with him. He whispered in some unknown tongue, but he sounded very urgent, as if he wished me to do something."

He leaned over and spoke to the mummy.

"Ra-Orkon, if you wish to speak to me, I am listening. I will try to understand."

A minute passed. Two. The only sound was a buzzing fly.

"Perhaps it was only my imagination after all," the professor said. "Yes, I'm sure it must have been. Bring me the small saw from the workshop, Wilkins. I'm going to cut a corner off the mummy case. My friend Jennings at the University of California will try to place the date when Ra-Orkon was buried by using the radioactive-carbon dating test on the wood."

"Very good, sir." The butler went out.

Professor Yarborough moved around the mummy case, tapping it, deciding just where to cut off the piece of wood he needed. In one place he thought he detected a slightly hollow sound, in another an apparent looseness, as if dry rot had set in.

As he worked, he became aware of a low murmuring issuing from the mummy case. He stood upright, looked startled, then placed his ear near the mummy's mouth.

The mummy was whispering to him! Words were issuing from the slightly parted lips—words spoken by an Egyptian who had been dead for three thousand years.

He could not understand the words. They were harsh and hissing syllables, in such a low voice he could barely hear them. But they rose and fell and seemed to be getting more and more urgent, as if the mummy were anxious to make him understand something.

Tremendous excitement gripped the professor. The language was probably ancient Arabic—here and there he felt he could almost understand a word.

"Go on, Ra-Orkon!" he urged. "I'm trying to understand."

"I beg your pardon, sir?"

At the words from behind him, the professor whirled. Ra-Orkon fell silent. Wilkins was standing there, holding a small, sharp saw.

"Wilkins!" Yarborough cried. "The mummy was whispering again! He started as soon as you left the room and ceased when you entered!"

Wilkins looked grave. He frowned.

"It's as if he won't speak unless you are alone, sir," he suggested. "Could you understand what he was saying?"

"No," the other man groaned. "Almost, but not quite. I'm not a language expert. He may be speaking in ancient Arabic, or in some form of Hittite or Chaldean speech."

Wilkins glanced out the window. His gaze fell on a house on the opposite slope of the canyon—a new, white stucco house perched on the hillside.

"Your friend, Professor Freeman, sir," he said. He pointed to the house. "He's our greatest authority on the languages of the Middle East. He could be here in five minutes, and if Ra-Orkon will speak for him, he might be able to tell you what Ra-Orkon is saying."

"Of course!" Professor Yarborough exclaimed. "I should have called him immediately. After all, his father was with me when I found Ra-Orkon. Poor chap —he was murdered a week later in the bazaars. Go and telephone Freeman, Wilkins. Ask him to come at once."

"Yes, sir." The butler had hardly left the room before the uncanny whispering began again.

Professor Yarborough made another futile attempt to understand what the mummy was saying, then gave up in despair. He looked through the open French window, across the canyon that separated him from the home of his younger friend, Professor Freeman. He could see Freeman's house, which was built on a steep slope far below the level of the road.

Yarborough watched his young friend leave his house by a side door, climb up a flight of stairs to his garage, and drive out a moment later onto the narrow road around the rim of the canyon. While Yarborough's eyes were anxiously watching his friend, his ears were straining to hear the whisper.

Once the mummy fell silent, great anxiety gripped the little man. Was the mummy going to stop just when there was a chance that someone might help interpret what it was saying?

"Keep talking, Ra-Orkon!" Professor Yarborough urged. "Please don't stop. I'm listening, I'm trying to understand."

After a moment the whispering resumed. Then the

professor heard a car stop outside. Presently a door opened and someone entered the room.

"Is that you, Freeman?" he asked.

"Yes, Yarborough, what is it?" A low, pleasant voice answered.

"Come here quietly. I want you to hear something." Then he felt the other man at his side.

"Ra-Orkon!" Yarborough cried. "Keep on! Don't stop now!"

But the mummy remained as silent as it must have been for thirty centuries before it had entered that room.

"I don't understand," Professor Freeman said as the older man turned. Freeman was a slender man of middle height, with a good-humored face, and hair just beginning to gray. "You seemed to be listening to the mummy talk just now."

"I was!" Yarborough cried. "He was whispering to me in some unknown language and I hoped you could interpret it for me. But he stopped as soon as he saw you. Or——"

He himself stopped, aware of the strange look his scientific friend was giving him.

"You don't believe it, do you?" he asked. "You don't believe that Ra-Orkon was whispering to me?"

Professor Freeman rubbed his chin.

"It is hard to believe," he said at last. "Of course, if I could hear him myself——"

"Let's try," Yarborough said. "Ra-Orkon, speak

again. We will try to understand."

Both men waited. The mummy remained silent.

"It's no use," Professor Yarborough sighed. "He was whispering, I assure you of it. But he won't speak unless I am alone with him. And I did hope you could hear him and interpret his speech."

Professor Freeman tried to look as if he believed his friend, but it was obvious that he found the story difficult to credit.

"I'd certainly like to help you if I could," he said. Then he caught sight of the small saw in the other's hand. "What is the saw for?" he asked, "Surely you weren't going to saw Ra-Orkon open!"

"No, no," Professor Yarborough said. "Merely wanted to saw off a corner of the case for a carbon dating test to determine when Ra-Orkon was buried."

"Damage such a valuable relic!" the young man exclaimed. "I hope that won't be necessary."

"I'm not sure Ra-Orkon and his case are valuable," Professor Yarborough said. "Merely mysterious. In any case, the carbon dating is necessary. But I'll put it off until I can solve the mystery of this curious whispering. Frankly, Freeman, at this point I am puzzled. A mummy can't whisper! But this one does. And only to me."

"Mmmm." Professor Freeman frowned, trying to hide a look of pity for the older man. "Well now, would you like me to keep old Ra-Orkon at my place for a few days? Alone with me, he might talk some more. Then I might be able to understand him and tell you what he says."

Professor Yarborough shot a keen glance toward the younger man.

"Thank you, Freeman," he said with dignity. "I can see you are just humoring me. You believe I have been imagining all this. Well, perhaps I have. I will keep Ra-Orkon here until I am sure whether or not it is merely my imagination."

Professor Freeman merely nodded.

"If you can get old Ra-Orkon to talk again," he said kindly, "call me at once. I'll drop whatever I'm doing and come over. Now I have to hurry. I have a conference at the university."

He bade Yarborough good-bye and left. Alone, the professor waited. Ra-Orkon remained silent. Presently Wilkins entered.

"Shall I serve your dinner, sir?"

"Yes, Wilkins." Professor Yarborough replied. "And remember, you must say nothing to anyone of what has happened."

"I understand, sir."

"Freeman's reaction tells me what my scientific colleagues would say if they heard I claimed a mummy was whispering to me. They would say I was getting old and senile. And imagine if the story got into the newspapers! My whole reputation as a scientist would be ruined."

"Indeed it would, sir," Wilkins agreed.

"Yet I must talk this over with someone." Yarborough compressed his lips. "Someone who is not a scientist yet who knows that there are many mysteries in the world. I have it. Tonight I'll call on my old friend Alfred Hitchcock and tell him. At least he won't scoff at me!"

Alfred Hitchcock did not scoff. Instead, as we have seen, he wrote a letter to The Three Investigators.

Chapter 3

Jupiter Tries Mind Reading

"HOW CAN A MUMMY WHISPER?" Pete repeated his earlier question. Bob could only shake his head. Both boys had read the letter twice. They would have thought it was a joke, except for the fact that it had come from Alfred Hitchcock, who assured them that his friend, Professor Yarborough, was badly upset by the mystery of the whispering mummy. Did The Three Investigators, Mr. Hitchcock asked, think they could help him?

"In fact," Pete went on, scowling, "how can a mummy talk at all?" He ran his fingers through his dark-brown hair. "I mean, a mummy is a mummy. It isn't human. That is, it was human, but it's not——"

"It's not alive," Bob put in. "What you don't like is the idea that all mummies are dead, but here's one that can talk."

"You bet I don't like it!" Pete said emphatically. He took back the letter and studied it. "Professor Robert Yarborough," he said. "An eminent Egyptol——Egyptol——"

"Egyptologist."

"Egyptologist. Lives in Hunter Canyon near Holly-wood. Has a private museum. Has a mummy that whispers to him but he can't understand it. Is slowly getting very nervous from the strain of it. Well, I don't blame him. I'm getting a little nervous just hearing about it! I don't want to get mixed up with any talking mummies. We've been entangled in too many weird mysteries already. Let's give our nerves a chance to calm down. Let's go over to Santa Monica and help that lady find her lost Abyssinian cat."

Bob Andrews picked up the other letter, the one from Mrs. Banfry.

"You know which case Jupe will want to tackle, don't you?" he asked.

"I know," Pete scowled. "The minute he reads the letter from Mr. Hitchcock, he'll be telephoning the Rent-'n-Ride Auto Rental Co. to send Worthington and the car so we can call on Professor Yarborough. But let's outvote him. We have two votes to his one. We'll vote to solve the mystery of the missing cat first."

"Jupe is awfully hard to outvote," Bob said. "We tried that once, when we were investigating Terror Castle, and you know what happened."

"I know," Pete agreed gloomily.

"Where is he, anyway? He ought to be back by now."

"Let's have a look around," Pete suggested. "Up periscope!"

He rose and strode across the tiny room to the corner. What seemed to be an ordinary length of small diameter stove pipe, ran up through the roof of the trailer. It ended in an elbow, and had two small pipes attached to it for handles. Looked at closely, it resembled the lower end of a submarine periscope—which was not surprising, for it actually was a crude but efficient periscope Jupiter had made the previous week.

Headquarters was still a secret to the outside world, hidden as it was by artfully placed piles of salvage materials. However, one drawback to the secrecy had become apparent. No one could see the hidden trailer, but once the boys were inside, they could not see out.

Jupiter had remedied this by building the periscope, which he named the "See-All." Made out of stove pipe with mirrors installed at angles in it, it rose through the roof close to the ventilating hatch. Anyone looking at it would see only an ordinary stove pipe.

Pete Crenshaw, tall and muscular, now worked the See-All up slowly, until the top of it cleared the highest piece of junk outside. Then he rotated it, walking around in a circle as he surveyed the entire scene outside.

"Mrs. Jones is selling some pipe to a plumber," he reported. "Hans is stacking second-hand lumber in the corner. And there's Jupe." Pete steadied the periscope. "He's walking his bike back from town. Must have had trouble——Yep, his front tire is flat."

"Probably ran over a nail," Bob suggested. "That's

what took him so long. Does he look grouchy?"

"No, he's listening to a transistor radio and smiling," Pete observed. "That's funny. I mean, Jupe hates to have things go wrong—even a flat tire. He takes it as a reflection on his efficiency. Jupe likes to plan ahead so everything goes as smooth as silk."

"Jupe is pretty terrific at planning," Bob said. "I just wish he wouldn't use such long words when he talks. Sometimes even I have trouble understanding him."

"Who doesn't?" Pete retorted. He turned the See-All slightly as he followed the view outside. "Now Jupe is wheeling his bike inside the main gate. He's giving something to Mrs. Jones. She's pointing this way and nodding. I guess she's telling him we're in the workshop."

"Now he's going into the office," Pete said. "I wonder what's taking him so long?" he fretted. "Oh, here he comes now."

"We'll have some fun with Jupe," Bob said. "I'll keep the letter from Alfred Hitchcock in my pocket. We'll show him the letter about Mrs. Banfry's missing cat and get him all worked up about finding it. Then we'll show him the letter Mr. Hitchcock sent about Professor Yarborough and his whispering mummy."

"And we'll say, of course, that we can't work on that case until after we find the cat!" Pete grinned. "I have another idea. Play along with me. It's my turn to make some deductions."

They waited. Outside they heard Jupe moving the iron grille which hid the mouth of Tunnel Two, the large galvanized pipe which was their main entrance into Headquarters.

Swiftly Pete Crenshaw lowered the periscope and took his seat at the desk. He and Bob heard the muffled sound of someone crawling through Tunnel Two, then the special rap on the trap door. Following this, the trapdoor lifted and Jupiter emerged into the trailer.

Jupiter Jones was a stocky, heavily built boy with black hair and piercing dark eyes. His round features were pink and boyish, but when he held himself erect and set his chin, he could look quite a bit older than he was. He could also let himself go limp, and seem both fat and very, very stupid—an ability which often fooled people into seriously underestimating him.

"Whew!" he puffed. "It's hot out!"

"Bad morning to have a flat tire," Pete said.

Jupe looked at him. "How do you know I had a flat tire?"

"Deduction," Pete said. "Bob and I have been boning up on deduction, like you told us to. Haven't we, Bob?"

Bob nodded. "Sure," he said. "Had to walk quite a way, wheeling your bike, didn't you, Jupe?"

Jupe eyed them warily. "Yes," he said. "I did. Now I'll be most interested if you will explain your deductions. Just so I can check on your cerebral processes."

"On our what?" Pete asked.

"Our thinking," Bob put in. "You tell him."

"Oh, sure," Pete said. "Hold out your hands."

Jupiter held out his hands. They were dirty, and on one palm was an imprint which could have been made by the tread of a bicycle tire.

"Well, go on," he said.

"Your right knee," Pete added. "It's dusty. Obviously you kneeled in the dust to examine something. Your hands are dirty and one has a bicycle tread mark on it. Deduction: you knelt down to examine your bike tire. This indicates you had a flat. Your shoes are very dusty, so you must have walked a long way. Elementary, my dear Jupe."

It really would have been a good piece of deduction if they had not actually known in advance that he had a flat tire. Jupiter appeared impressed.

"Very good," he said. "Such ability should not be wasted in looking for a lost cat."

"What?" Pete and Bob exclaimed.

"I said such advanced ability in the art of deductive reasoning and ratiocination should not be wasted in pursuit of an Abyssinian cat that has vanished from its usual haunts," Jupe said, deliberately throwing in a lot of long words, which Pete hated.

"In fact, investigators of your ability should be after bigger game such as——" He paused, as if thinking hard——"such as the mystery of a 3,000-year-old mummy that whispers cryptic messages in an unknown language to its owner."

"How do you know about the whispering mummy?" Pete almost shouted.

"While you have been boning up on deduction," Jupiter said, "I have been boning up on mind reading. In your pocket, Bob, you have a letter giving Professor Yarborough's address. I have already phoned for the car and Worthington. They will be here in ten minutes. Then we will call on the professor and offer our aid in his problem of the mummy that insists on whispering to him."

Speechless, Pete and Bob stared at him in stunned amazement.

Chapter 4

The Curse of the Mummy

"HOW DID YOU KNOW about the letter from Mr. Hitchcock, telling us about Professor Yarborough and his whispering mummy?" Pete demanded half an hour later for the fifth time.

Jupiter Jones sighed. "If you don't believe I'm a mind reader, you will have to figure it out for yourself," he said. "Use your power of deduction. When I entered Headquarters you were doing some remarkable deduction about my flat tire. Simply continue the good work."

This answer reduced Pete to frustrated silence. Bob Andrews grinned to himself. Jupe had got the better of them again. In his own good time he would tell them how. For the moment, Bob was happy to be in on the start of what might be—and indeed, was going to turn out to be—a mystery eerie and baffling enough to intrigue any investigator.

The three boys occupied the rear seat of the big,

ancient Rolls Royce sedan, which was their present means of transportation over the sizable distances that prevail in Southern California. They were now rolling smoothly through the hills that separate Rocky Beach from the northern section of Hollywood.

"Jupe," Bob said, stretching luxuriously, "I don't know what we'll do when your thirty days' use of this car is up. We've used it for fourteen days already."

"Fifteen, I regret to say, Master Andrews," Worthington, the tall, erect English chauffeur in the front seat reminded him. A warm friendship had sprung up between him and the boys. "Counting today, that is. I will miss our little adventures when I no longer have the pleasure of driving you."

"That just leaves fifteen days," Pete sighed.

"Two and two don't always make four," Jupe said, his manner mysterious. "And fifteen and fifteen don't always make thirty. Stop here, please, Worthington."

The car stopped a few feet below the crest of one of the many ridges in the hills around Hollywood. A driveway turned off from the road, and large stone pillars stood on each side of it. A metal plate bearing the name Yarborough was bolted to one pillar.

The driveway ran down the canyon slope into an extensive estate covered with many trees. Just visible through the trees and shrubs was the red-tile roof of a mansion built in the old Spanish style. Beyond the mansion the ground dipped much more steeply to the bottom of the canyon; then it climbed up to the next ridge. On the opposite slope there were a number of homes built on various levels.

"That must be Professor Yarborough's home," Jupiter said to the others. "I telephoned, and he's expecting us, so drive on down, Worthington, and we'll introduce ourselves. I'm very anxious to meet that mummy. Maybe he'll speak to us!"

"He'd better not!" Pete muttered. "I don't stay in the same room with any mummy that talks. Personally, I don't blame the professor for being upset."

Professor Yarborough was at that moment very upset. He was sitting in an easy chair on the terrace, sipping the hot consommé Wilkins had just served him.

"Tell me, Wilkins," he asked anxiously, "did you listen again last night as I asked you to?"

"Yes, sir," the butler answered. "I stayed in the room with Ra-Orkon until it was quite dark. Once I thought I heard something——"

"Yes, yes? Go on!"

"But I was forced to conclude it was just imagination, sir." The butler took away the empty cup and handed his employer a napkin. Professor Yarborough wiped his lips.

"Something's happened to me, Wilkins," he said. "I find myself waking up at night, my heart pounding. This mystery—it is unnerving me."

"I find it very upsetting myself, sir," Wilkins responded. "Do you suppose——"

"Do I suppose what? Speak up, Wilkins!"

"I was only going to say, sir, that I wondered if you had thought of returning Ra-Orkon to the Egyptian government. Then, sir, you would be free of this distressing——"

"No!" Professor Yarborough's lips set in a stubborn line. "There is a great deal here that I don't understand. I refuse to give up before I know what it all means. I think I'll be getting some help soon."

"A detective, sir?" Wilkins exclaimed. "But I thought you did not want any word of this occurrence to reach the police."

"Not the police. Some investigators my friend Alfred Hitchcock recommended." A sound of melodious chimes echoed inside the house behind them. "That may be them now. Please hurry, Wilkins, and bring them out here at once."

"Yes, sir." The butler went into the house and returned leading three boys onto the terrace—one stocky and black-haired, one tall and muscular, one slight, wearing glasses, who had a brace on his leg and limped a little. The professor frowned.

Jupiter Jones saw the frown and knew what it meant. Professor Yarborough had expected them to be older. Jupe drew himself up straight and set his chin so that he immediately looked older. From his pocket he whipped out a business card. The professor took it automatically. It read:

THE THREE INVESTIGATORS

"We Investigate Anything"

? ? ?

First Investigator: Jupiter Jones
Second Investigator: Peter Crenshaw
Records and Research: Bob Andrews

The professor asked the question that almost everyone asked.

"What are the question marks for?" he inquired. "They would seem to indicate a doubt of your ability."

Bob and Pete grinned at each other. The question marks were Jupe's idea. A question mark was their secret symbol. When one of them wanted to let the others know that he had been to a certain place, he chalked up a question mark. Jupiter used white chalk, Bob green, and Pete blue so each of them always knew who had left the mark.

"The question mark," Jupiter said now in his most adult manner, "otherwise known as the interrogation mark, is a universal symbol for a question unanswered, a riddle unsolved, a mystery unexplained. Therefore we have made it our trademark. We will undertake to solve any mystery you want us to tackle. We cannot promise success, but we can promise to try."

"Hmmm." The man in the chair turned the card in his fingers thoughtfully. "If you hadn't made that last statement, I would have had Wilkins show you out. No one can promise success in any endeavor, as I well know. But success often follows a good try."

He paused, studying them. Finally he nodded.

"Alfred Hitchcock sent you to me," he said. "I have faith in his judgment. I can't call in the police for obvious reasons. I can't ask a private detective to help me —he'd think I had bats in my belfry, I believe the phrase is. A professional colleague would just secretly pity me and spread the report that I was old and senile. But three imaginative boys, with no preconceived notions—— Yes, I have a feeling that if anyone can help me get to the bottom of this thing, you can."

He rose from his chair and walked toward the left wing of the house.

"Come along," he said. "I will introduce you to Ra-Orkon and we can get started."

Jupe followed him. Pete and Bob were about to, but Wilkins held out his hand to stop them. The butler's hand was shaking. His face showed strain and anxiety.

"Boys," he said, "before you become involved with the mummy, Ra-Orkon, there's something you should know."

"What's that?" Pete asked, frowning.

"There's a curse on it," Wilkins said, lowering his voice. "There was a curse put on its tomb and anyone who entered it or disturbed Ra-Orkon. Over the years the curse has taken the lives of almost all the members of the original expedition. Violently. Unexpectedly.

"The professor won't admit it. He won't admit anything that isn't scientific. And it has never affected him —until now. But now he actually has the mummy in the house here and I—I'm afraid. For him. And for myself. And for you boys too, if you get mixed up in this."

Wide-eyed, they stared at him. Wilkins' face worked with emotion. He was obviously sincere. At that moment, Jupe turned.

"Come on," he called. "What are you waiting for?"

They hurried after him and stepped into the big museum room through the open French window. The professor was striding directly to the wooden mummy case. He lifted off the lid and pointed.

"There is Ra-Orkon," he said. "And I hope—I do hope you can help me learn what it is he is trying to tell me."

The mahogany-colored mummy of Ra-Orkon seemed to be resting peacefully inside its case. Its eyes were closed as always, yet they looked almost as if they might open.

Jupiter examined the mummy with a keen professional interest. Bob and Pete, however, felt themselves breathing a bit hard. It wasn't that the mummy was unpleasant to look at. It was the idea. A whispering mummy was eerie enough to think about. But a whispering mummy that had a curse on it——

Bob's eyes met Pete's. Pete looked miserable.

"Gleeps!" Pete said under his breath. "Jupe's really got us into something this time!"

Chapter 5

Sudden Danger

JUPITER JONES was studying the mummy of Ra-Orkon intently. Professor Yarborough patted his forehead with a handkerchief.

"Wilkins," he said to the butler, "open the windows. You know I can't stand being in a closed room."

"Yes, sir." The tall butler pushed the French windows open, and a breeze swept into the room, making the masks on the wall rustle and tinkle.

Jupiter looked up at the sound.

"That wasn't what you heard, Professor?" he asked. "A sound made by the breeze perhaps?"

"No, no, my boy, " the man said. "I know the difference between casual sounds and human speech! The mummy was definitely whispering."

"Then we will rule out the possibility that you were mistaken," Jupiter said. "We will proceed on the assumption that you actually heard speech, possibly in ancient Arabic, possibly not."

"Is there anything else I can do, sir?" Wilkins asked.

"Or shall I resume my duties?"

All of them looked at him. They saw his eyes widen in sudden alarm. Then he hurled himself upon Professor Yarborough.

"Look out, sir," he yelled. "Look out!"

The two men fell to the floor. An instant later the tall, wooden statue of Annubis, the jackal-headed god that had been standing by the open window, crashed forward almost upon the spot where the professor had been standing. It rolled over on its side and the jackal face seemed to snarl at him.

Shakily, Professor Yarborough and Wilkins rose. They looked down at the fallen statue.

"I saw it tottering, sir," Wilkin's voice trembled. "I knew it was going to fall. It might have struck you and injured you badly." He swallowed hard. "It's the curse of Ra-Orkon, sir," he said. "It has followed the mummy here."

"Nonsense!" the Professor said, dusting himself off. "The curse is just a newspaper story. That inscription on the tomb didn't mean at all what Lord Carter thought it did. It's just chance that the statue of Annubis should fall the way it did."

"That statue has stood without falling for three thousand years," Wilkins said in a husky whisper. "Why should it fall now? You might have been seriously injured, or even killed as Lord Carter was when——"

"Lord Carter was killed in an automobile accident!" the professor snapped. "You may go, Wilkins."

"Yes, sir." The butler turned, but Jupiter halted him. Jupiter had been bending over the statue, and now he looked up.

"Wilkins, you said you saw the statue start to topple," he stated. "Please tell us just exactly how it moved."

"It began to lean forward, Master Jones," Wilkins said. "When I saw it, it was already leaning at a dangerous angle. As if—as if planning to injure the professor."

"Wilkins!" his employer said sharply.

"It's true, sir. Annubis just leaned forward and—and fell. I acted as swiftly as I could. I—I'm glad I was in time."

"Yes, I'm very grateful," the professor snapped. "But let's have no more talk about curses."

As he said the word "curses," they all jumped. A golden mask had fallen from the wall and thudded to the floor behind them.

"You—you see, sir?" Wilkins asked, his pallor increasing.

"The breeze," the professor said, but with less assurance. "It blew Annubis over and blew down the mask."

Jupiter, crouched over the wooden statue, was running his hand along the square base on which it had stood.

"It's pretty heavy, sir," he said. "And the base isn't warped or anything. It would take quite a breeze to blow over this statue."

"Young man," Professor Yarborough told him, "I am a scientist. I do not believe in curses or evil spirits. If you are going to assist me, I must ask you to remember that."

Jupiter straightened, his face thoughtful.

"I don't believe in them either, sir," he said. "But the fact remains that two curious incidents have occurred, without any apparent cause, inside of five minutes."

"Mere chance," the professor told him. "Now, young man, you said you believed the mummy whispered to me as I have stated. Perhaps you have a theory about how a long-dead mummy can whisper?"

Jupiter Jones pinched his lower lip. Bob and Pete knew the gesture meant he was throwing his mental gears into high.

"I have a theory, sir."

"A scientific theory?" Professor Yarborough demanded, his white goatee moving as he bit off the words. "Not hocus-pocus?"

"Yes, sir. A very scientific theory." Jupe turned to Pete and Bob. "Pete, you and Bob might go ask Worthington to give you the leather bag that's in the trunk of the car. It has some equipment in it that I want to try out."

"Sure, Jupe!" Pete exclaimed, glad to have a chance to get out. "Come on, Bob."

"I will show you through the house," Wilkins offered.

They left Jupiter and the professor alone in the museum room and followed Wilkins down a long hall which led to the front door. The Rolls Royce was parked outside. Worthington, as usual when not otherwise occupied, was carefully polishing the shining exterior of the car.

"Boys," the butler whispered as he let them out the door, "the professor is very stubborn. He won't admit there is a curse. But you saw what happened. Next time he may be killed. Or one of us, maybe. Please persuade him to send Ra-Orkon back to Egypt!"

Then he vanished, leaving them in a thoughtful frame of mind.

"Maybe Jupe doesn't believe in curses," Pete said. "And I'm not saying I do. But something tells me that if we knew what was good for us, we'd get out of here!"

Bob Andrews had no ready answer. He didn't believe in ancient curses, either. On the other hand, suppose there was something to it?

Worthington looked up as they approached.

"All finished, lads?" he asked.

"Just getting started," Pete told him, his tone gloomy. "This time we're tangling with an ancient Egyptian curse, and there's no telling what will happen. Right now we need the leather case Jupe put in the trunk."

"I'll back Master Jones against an Egyptian curse anytime," Worthington said, leading the way to the rear of the car. He opened the trunk and took out a flat leather case.

"This must be what Master Jones wants," he said. "He asked me to put it in without telling anyone."

Pete took the case and they started back to the museum room.

"Wonder what's in it?" he speculated, hefting the case. "It's pretty heavy. Jupe has been planning to surprise us, I bet."

"He's getting back at us for pretending to deduce he had a flat tire," Bob said.

They entered the museum room. Jupe and Professor Yarborough had lifted the statue of the jackal-headed Annubis back into place. Jupe was pushing it with his hand. Then he shook his head.

"It would take a gale to blow this statue over, sir," he said, as Bob and Pete entered. "Definitely no breeze could do it."

The professor drew his bushy brows together.

"Are you saying a supernatural force was at work?"

"I don't know what caused the statue to fall, Professor," Jupiter said politely. "But I'll show you how to make the mummy whisper."

He took the case Pete handed him and unlocked it. Throwing back the lid, he revealed what looked like three oversized transistor radios.

Jupiter did not like to give explanations when he could demonstrate instead. Now he handed one of the radios to Pete. From the case he took a leather belt with copper wire sewed to it, and fastened this around Pete's waist. He plugged in a lead-in wire from the belt to the little radio and handed it to Pete.

"Open the window and walk out on the terrace, then through the gardens," he said. "Hold the radio to your ear and pretend to be listening to it. But press this button on the side and talk instead. To listen, let up on the button."

"But what is it" Pete demanded.

"It's a walkie-talkie," Jupiter said. "The copper belt is your antenna. It has a sending and receiving range of half a mile, using the Citizen's Band for transmission. I decided we needed some way to keep in touch with each other if we ever got separated on a case, so I started making these last week."

"I walk down through the garden and talk," Pete repeated. "What do I say?"

"Anything you want," Jupiter told him. "Open the window and go straight down."

"Well, okay," Pete agreed. He shot a glance at the First Investigator. "So this is how you did your mind reading!" he blurted out.

"We'll talk about that later," Jupe grinned. "Right now I want to demonstrate for the professor. Start talking when you get—let's see. . ." He opened the tall French window and looked out. "Oh, down by that wall with the big stone ball on top of the gatepost."

"Okay." Pete started out across the tiled terrace, holding the radio to his ear.

"Now, Professor, if you don't mind my touching the mummy——" Jupiter began.

"Not at all, my boy," the professor said. "Just be gentle with him."

Jupiter bent over the mummy case. In a moment he straightened. In his hand he held one of the three walkie-talkies. The third had vanished.

"All right," he said into the little radio. "Start talking, Pete. Professor, you and Bob listen."

They all listened. The silence was broken by an indistinct murmur.

"Bend over the mummy case," Jupiter suggested. He himself was still holding the second little walkie-talkie to his ear.

Frowning, the professor bent over the mummy case. Bob also leaned over. And they heard the mummy whispering!

They quickly realized, however, that the mummy was whispering in Pete's voice.

"I'm past the wall now," Pete was saying. "I'm walking straight down the slope toward a big clump of bushes."

"Keep going, Second," Jupiter said into his radio. To the others in the room with him he said, "You see, it's quite simple to make a mummy whisper."

He turned back a loose fold of the linen wrapping, which the professor had removed from Ra-Orkon's face. Under the wrapping was the third walkie-talkie. From it was coming Pete's voice. The effect, however, was a very convincing one and they could easily have believed the mummy was whispering if they had not known the truth.

"A scientific solution, sir," Jupiter told the professor. "A small radio receiver hidden with the mummy, and someone broadcasting into it from outside the house would easily give you the effect——"

At that moment, Pete's voice, coming to them from the tiny radio, took on a note of alarm.

"Oh oh!" he said. "There's somebody hiding in the bushes ahead of me. It's a boy. He doesn't know I saw him. I'm going to grab him."

"Wait a minute!" Jupiter said urgently. "We'll help you."

"If you do he'll run away," Pete's voice came back to them. "I'm going to pretend to be wandering around, then I'll jump him. As soon as you hear me yell, come running."

"All right, Pete," Jupiter said. "You grab him and we'll come help." He turned to the professor. "An intruder lurking outside," he said. "This may solve the mystery—if we can nab him."

"I wonder what's happening out there?" Bob wriggled with impatience. "Pete's not transmitting now. I wish we could see."

They waited. The silence continued.

Pete was moving around the garden on the steep slope below the house, fiddling with the radio at his ear and seeming not to notice the almost invisible form that was hidden in the shrubbery. Slowly he moved toward the bushes. Then, when it was too late for the boy hidden there to take flight, he rushed the hiding place. A slender boy, about Bob's size, with olive skin and very black eyes, leaped up. Pete crashed against him and they went down in a tangle of arms and legs.

"I've got him!" Pete yelled into the radio just before he leaped. As they came together, the boy shouted out a string of words in some strange tongue. Then the little walkie-talkie was knocked from Pete's hand and crushed beneath them as the two rolled down the slope. The strange boy was fighting furiously to get away.

The boy was slender, but he was as lithe and slippery as an eel. No sooner did Pete get a grip on him than he broke free and was almost gone. Just in time Pete grappled him again and they went tumbling across the sloping lawn, winding up against a stone wall.

Once more the boy shouted a series of strange words. Pete didn't waste any breath on words. He only hoped Jupe and Bob were coming fast!

They were coming, and Professor Yarborough with them. When they heard Pete's shout over the walkie-talkie in the mummy case, Bob ran for the door. Despite his limp he got there first, with Jupe and the professor on his heels.

Down below they saw the furious tussle. But before they could get across the terrace, someone else had entered the scene. This was a workman in blue overalls who ran toward the two below, dropping a shovel as he ran.

"It's one of the Magasay brothers, who do my gardening," the Professor said swiftly. "They're Filipinos. There are seven of them and I can never tell them apart, but they're all Judo experts. They're small, but they're very wiry, you know. He'll be able to help better than we can."

They slowed down a bit. The gardener ran down the slope and bent over the two boys. He flung an arm around the throat of the strange boy and lifted him kicking and struggling off Pete.

"I have intruder," he called in a marked accent. "I hold him tight."

Pete got slowly to his feet. The kicking, struggling boy had swung the man around in his efforts to get away.

"Watch him, he's a wildcat!" Pete said.

The other boy grunted something in his strange tongue. Mr. Magasay shouted at him.

"Hold still. Not make me hurt you!" Then in his excitement he rattled off a string of foreign words. In the middle of them he gave a shriek, the boy darted away, over the wall, down the slope, and into the underbrush below before Pete could even move.

At that moment Jupiter and Professor Yarborough reached them, with Bob behind.

"What happened?" the professor cried. "How did he get away?"

The gardener turned. "I foolish," he said. "Biting not part of Judo so I do not think of it."

He held out his right hand. A series of tooth marks made a line on the back and blood was trickling out of them. The strange boy had bitten deeply and savagely to get away.

"You did your best," "Professor Yarborough said. "Go see the doctor immediately and have that hand dressed. Don't risk infection."

"Sorry so stupid," the gardener said.

He backed away and started around the house to where his truck was parked. Like many gardeners in Southern California, he and his brothers were independent businessmen who took care of several estates, driving from one to another.

Pete was still trying to get his breath back.

"Gosh," he said in disappointment. "I thought we had him."

"I wonder who he is?" Bob said. "What was he doing here?"

"Spying on the house from the bushes," Pete said. "I saw him move. That's when I spoke to you."

"He undoubtedly could have told us a great deal," Jupiter said, pinching his lip.

"Boys," Professor Yarborough said, "I don't know what to make of this——"

They turned toward him expectantly.

"——but just after Pete tackled him, we heard the boy shout something which came clearly over the radio before it got smashed."

"Some foreign language," Pete agreed.

"It was modern Arabic," Professor Yarborough told them. "And what the boy called out was, 'I pray to the noble spirit of Ra-Orkon to come to my aid!' "

Jupiter started to say something, but his words were cut off by Pete's shout.

"Look out!" Pete yelled and pointed.

They swung around swiftly and gazed with sudden alarm up the slope.

One of the huge granite balls, weighing at least a ton apiece, on top of the pillars at either side of the gate, had rolled from its place.

Now, gathering speed, it was bounding toward them.

Chapter 6

A Surprising Visitor

AS THE GREAT STONE BALL bounded toward them, Bob
and Pete prepared to run. The professor's sharp cry
halted them.

"Stand still!" he called. "Don't move an inch."

Jupiter's respect for Professor Yarborough increased.
The professor had seen, even before Jupiter did, that
the slope of the ground would cause the granite ball
to miss them.

It did so, turning in its course and bumping past
them ten feet away to crash against a clump of euca-
lyptus trees further down the slope.

"Wow!" Bob mopped his forehead. "I was going to
duck right over in that direction."

"Not me," Pete said. "I was heading out of here.
That thing must weigh a ton."

"Slightly more," Professor Yarborough said. "A ball
of granite that size, containing a cubic footage of—let
me see. . ."

"Professor!"

They looked up. Wilkins, the butler, was rushing down toward them from the house.

"I saw from the kitchen window what happened," he panted. "Are you all right?"

"Yes, yes," the white-haired man said impatiently. "As you can see. And I know what you're going to say. But don't say it. I forbid you to."

"I must, sir," Wilkins answered. "It's the curse of Ra-Orkon. That's what made the accident happen. Ra-Orkon will kill you, sir. He may kill all of us!"

"The curse of Ra-Orkon?" Jupiter's eyes lighted. "Is there a curse on the mummy, Professor Yarborough?"

"No, no, certainly not," the professor said. "You're too young to remember, but when I first discovered the tomb in the Valley of the Kings, the newspapers ran a lot of ridiculous stories about a certain inscription . . ."

"It said, 'Woe to all who disturb the sleep of Ra-Orkon, The Just, who sleeps within,'" Wilkins stated, his voice shaking. "And one by one almost everyone in the original party has died or suffered severe injury because——"

"Wilkins!" the professor thundered. "You're forgetting yourself!"

"Yes, sir," said the butler, obviously agitated. "I'm sorry, sir."

"The inscription said," Professor Yarborough told Jupiter, " 'Ra-Orkon, The Just, sleeps within. Woe if his sleep be disturbed.' Meaning, woe to Ra-Orkon. It

is true that Lord Carter and I disagreed over the exact
wording of the inscription, but I know that I am correct."

He paused, then added, "It is also true some mystery
surrounds Ra-Orkon. Lord Carter and I discovered
him really by accident. His tomb was well hidden in a
rocky cliff. Inside were none of the usual relics found
in tombs of royalty. Nothing but the plain mummy
case with Ra-Orkon in it, and his favorite royal cat
mummified with him. No inscription telling who he
was, or what he had done, as was customary. It was
almost as if he had been buried in such a way that
he would attract no attention, or possibly as if his relatives intended to rebury him more magnificently
later. If any of the grave robbers of the time had discovered him, they wouldn't have gotten anything from
his tomb!

"However, the care with which he was embalmed
made it clear that he was no ordinary man. Yet we
cannot even get a date for his death. His name is confusing. The name *Ra* is associated with kings of earlier
dynasties. The *Orkon* part of his name suggests the
Libyan influence—the Libyans began to move into
Egypt slightly more than three thousand years ago and
eventually became the rulers of Egypt. I want to es-
tablish an exact date for his burial. Then I shall make
a close study to see if I can learn why he was buried
so plainly, and so secretly.

"As for what Wilkins said about harm coming to

the members of our party, you must not let Wilkins mislead you. Lord Carter died in an automobile accident. Aleph Freeman, a brilliant but self-taught man, my secretary and the father of my friend Professor Freeman, who lives over there"—he gestured toward the opposite slope—"was murdered in a Cairo bazaar. The photographer and Lord Carter's personal secretary were injured in the accident that killed Lord Carter but lived for many years afterward. The Egyptian overseer of the labor force died of a snake bite.

"It is only natural that in a quarter of a century a certain number of accidents should happen to the members of any given group, and some should die. Believe me—there is no curse!"

Pete and Bob looked at each other. They wanted to believe him, but it wasn't easy.

"Oh, there's one thing more," the professor said. "It can't have anything to do with this whispering, but last week, the very day Ra-Orkon arrived, a Libyan rug merchant, named Achmed Something-or-other, came and tried to persuade me to give Ra-Orkon to him. He said he represented the House of Hamid, in Libya, and Ra-Orkon was his employer's ancestor. Said it had been revealed in a vision by a magician. What nonsense! I sent the fellow off in a hurry. As the merchant left, he warned me that Ra-Orkon's spirit would give me trouble unless I allowed him to take Ra-Orkon back for proper burial by his family."

Pete and Bob exchanged still another glance. The

whole thing was sounding worse to them by the minute, even though Jupe looked very cheerful about the eeriness of the mystery.

"Now," the professor said, "let us forget about silly superstition and see why that ornamental concrete ball rolled off the gatepost."

He led the way up the slope to the stone gatepost atop which the granite ball had been set. They quickly saw that it had been held in place by a ring of mortar making a small collar for it to sit in. However, time and the weather seemed to have weakened the cement ring. On one side it had worn away. Furthermore, a settlement of the ground had caused the stone gatepost to lean a bit downhill.

"It's easy to see what happened," Professor Yarborough commented. "The weather wore away the retaining ring of mortar. The slight slope of the gatepost was just enough to let the ball roll off. Possibly a very mild earthquake tremor started it just now. We have dozens of such tiny tremors in this area every year, as we are situated over a major fault line."

Unconvinced and shaking his head, the butler left them. The others climbed back up to the terrace and entered the museum room, where they gathered around the mummy case of Ra-Orkon.

"You were very ingenious," the professor said to Jupiter, "in making the mummy whisper. However, your solution cannot be the correct one, for there is no radio hidden inside the mummy case."

"Have you looked, sir?" Jupiter asked respectfully. The professor blinked.

"Why, no," he said. "I suppose I should."

He removed the walkie-talkie Jupiter had put inside the linen folds that wrapped Ra-Orkon, then felt around to see if anything else was hidden. Finding nothing, he carefully lifted the mummy. They all could see nothing was beneath him.

Now it was Jupiter who began to look baffled. He began to inspect the mummy case itself—first the lid, then the case. He even tilted it slightly to look under it.

"No wires," he said finally. "No receiving set—nothing. I'm sorry, Professor, my first theory has proved wrong."

"First theories often do," the professor told him. "But I hope you will have a second theory that may explain the mummy's whispering."

"I do not have any theory at the moment, sir," Jupiter answered. "You say the mummy whispers to you only when you are alone?"

"Yes." The professor nodded. "And so far, only in the late afternoon."

Jupiter pinched his lip.

"Does anyone else occupy this house with you?" he asked.

"Only Wilkins. He has been in my employ for ten years. Before that he was an actor. In vaudeville, I think. A cleaning woman comes in three times a week, but Wilkins is both chef and chauffeur, as well as butler."

"What about the gardener?" Jupiter asked. "Does he happen to be a new employee?"

"Oh, no." The professor shook his head. "The Magasay brothers—I mentioned seven of them—have worked for me for eight years. Sometimes one comes, sometimes another, but not one of them has ever been inside this house."

"Mmm," Jupiter pondered, a scowl on his round features. Then he nodded. "Yes," he said, "I must hear the mummy whisper by myself."

"But apparently it will whisper only to me," the professor objected. "It would not whisper to Wilkins or to Professor Freeman."

"Yes," Bob piped up. "Why should it whisper to you, Jupe? Your're a total stranger to it."

"Now wait a minute, wait a minute," Pete protested. "I don't like this kind of talk, as if the mummy—well, as if it knew what was going on."

"It is not scientific," Professor Yarborough admitted. "Yet it almost seems as if somehow it does know."

Jupe looked confident. "I believe," he said, "that the mummy will whisper to me. Then I will have more information to work on. We will come back this evening, Professor, and make the test."

"Gosh, where is Jupe, anyway?" Pete demanded, looking at the electric clock on the wall of Headquarters later that afternoon. "It's a quarter past six, and he told us to meet him here at six o'clock sharp."

"Didn't he tell his aunt where he was going?" Bob asked, looking up from the notes he had been writing down about the morning's episode. He had been working all afternoon in the library, where he had a part-time job, and couldn't get at his special assignment earlier.

"No, he didn't," Pete said. "But he went off in the car with Worthington. Let's take a look and see if the car is in sight."

He strode to the See-All and elevated it.

"There it is now!" he exclaimed, peering into the eyepiece. "Coming down the road from town. Jupe's leaning out the window. Maybe he's trying to reach us on the walkie-talkie."

They hastened back to the desk. On the desk was the small loudspeaker which Jupiter had rigged up so when there was a telephone call they could all hear what was being said. Only, unknown to them, he had rebuilt it during the past week. It was now a walkie-talkie unit as well, and could transmit anything that was said in the office unless it was turned off.

"Jupe and his mind reading!" Pete growled as they seated themselves. "This morning he was listening to every word we said about the letters from Mr. Hitch-cock and Mrs. Banfry as he walked his bike home."

He leaned toward the loudspeaker and clicked a switch.

"This is Headquarters," he said. "Calling First Investigator. Can you read me, First Investigator?"

He clicked over the switch and a power hum sounded from the speaker. Over it came Jupiter's voice.

"This is First Investigator. I will join you as soon as I can. I note that you have been using the See-All. Lower it when it is not in use. Over and out."

"Heard and understood," Pete said and clicked off the speaker. Bob went over to the periscope.

"Jupe doesn't miss much," he said. "The car is coming in the gate and he's getting out. He's carrying a little zipper bag and heading this way. He'll be here in a minute. Worthington and the car are waiting."

He lowered the See-All and resumed his seat.

"I wonder where he went," he speculated. Then, as a few minutes passed and there was no sign of their partner, he added, "And I wonder what's keeping him? Do you suppose he got stuck in Tunnel Two?"

But at that moment they heard the special rap on the floor which told them one of their group was entering. The trap door rose and a head and shoulders appeared.

Pete and Bob stared down. Half inside the trailer was an elderly man who had bushy white hair, wore gold-rimmed glasses, and had a small white goatee.

"Professor Yarborough!" Pete yelped. "How did you get here? What's happened to Jupe?"

"The curse of Ra-Orkon has befallen him." The old man climbed into the tiny office with surprising agility.

"Ra-Orkon has changed him into me."

Then he swept off the white wig, the spectacles, and the small goatee and grinned at them.

"If I fooled you," he said, "I ought to be able to fool a mummy. Especially a mummy that has its eyes shut."

"Jupe!" Bob exclaimed.

"Gleeps, Jupe!" Pete said in bewilderment. "You did have us fooled. Why were you made up like Professor Yarborough?"

"As a test," Jupiter said as he finished climbing into Headquarters and put the wig, spectacles, and goatee into the zipper bag he was carrying. In the better light they could now see that some age lines had been drawn on his forehead and around his eyes with a make-up pencil to help make his youthful face seem much older.

"I went to see Mr. Grant," he said. "I told him what the professor looked like and he made me up."

Mr. Grant was a make-up specialist whom they had met during an earlier adventure. He was a wizard at altering the appearance of almost anyone.

"But why?" Bob wanted to know.

"To fool the mummy," Jupe said.

"To fool the mummy!" Pete yelled. "What does that mean?"

"If the mummy thinks I'm Professor Yarborough, perhaps it'll whisper to me," Jupiter told him. "Since apparently it won't whisper to anyone else."

"Now wait a minute!" Pete shouted. "The way

you're talking you'd think this mummy could see and hear as well as talk. Gosh, it's only a mummy. It's been dead for three thousand years. Anytime I'm on a case where somebody has to disguise himself to fool a mummy dead that long, I stop being on that case. I vote we forget the mummy and go looking for that lost cat."

Bob started to speak, swallowed, and stopped. Jupe was pinching his lip, looking thoughtful.

"Then you don't want to come with us now to see if I can get the mummy to whisper?" he asked.

Now it was Pete's turn to hesitate. He was already regretting his outburst. But he had uttered the words and, being normally stubborn, he was stuck with them. He gave a short nod.

"That's what I said," he grumbled. "Next time maybe the whole roof will fall in. That curse was certainly trying hard enough to get at us this morning."

"All right, Jupiter agreed. "Since there are three of us, there's no reason why we can't handle more than one case at a time. You go to interview Mrs. Banfry, the owner of the cat, and Bob and I will go to interview the mummy as planned. All right, Bob?"

Bob knew that Pete hadn't really expected Jupe to take him seriously, but Jupe was the head of the firm. As he said, there was no reason why they couldn't investigate more than one case at a time. So he nodded.

"Very well," Jupe said. "You'll just have time to get a first interview before dark, Pete. Since we'll have to use the Rolls Royce, ask Hans if he can drive you to Santa Monica in the small truck."

Pete hesitated. Then he said gruffly, "All right, Jupe. I'll do that."

He lifted the trap door, dropped through, and began crawling through Tunnel Two to the entrance behind the printing press in the workshop. He emerged and zigzagged his way through the piles of junk toward the office. Hans was just locking up, but agreed to drive Pete to Santa Monica.

Okay, he thought, he'd show Jupe. He'd find that lost cat while maybe First and Records were being demolished in some nasty way by the curse of Ra-Orkon. If that was what they wanted, let them have it!

Chapter 7

The Jackal God Appears

SLIGHTLY LESS than an hour later, Pete was in Santa Monica talking to excitable little Mrs. Banfry about her lost cat.

At almost the same time, at the home of Professor Yarborough, Jupiter Jones entered the museum room alone and turned on the overhead lights. It was still daylight outside, but as the sun had set behind the ridge of the canyon, deep twilight enveloped the big house.

Jupiter entered the room with the slow movements of an old man. He went directly to the French windows and swung them open. Then he moved to the wooden case which held the mummy of Ra-Orkon. He lifted off the top of the case and bent over and stared down at the still features of the mummy.

"Ra-Orkon," Jupiter said loudly. "Speak and I will listen. I will try to understand."

It was not in his natural voice that Jupiter spoke, but in quite a good imitation of Professor Yarborough's voice. Jupiter was wearing the wig, spectacles, and goatee provided for him by Mr. Grant, the make-up specialist. He was wearing one of the professor's linen coats and a tie of the professor's. As the professor was small and plump, and Jupiter was stocky, and muscular, it was not too difficult for the boy to make himself look very much like the famous Egyptologist.

In an adjoining room, Bob Andrews and the professor waited anxiously for the results of the test. Wilkins was busy in the kitchen and knew nothing of the impersonation.

Jupiter leaned over the mummy case and said once more: "Great Ra-Orkon, speak to me. Make me understand."

Was that a murmur he heard? He turned his head to hear better, and now he heard words. Strange, harsh words in no language he had ever heard before, delivered in a sibilant whisper.

Startled, Jupiter jerked his head up and looked around the room. He was totally alone. The door into the room where the professor and Bob waited was shut.

He brought his ear again close to the unmoving lips of the mummy and the whispering continued, urgent, commanding. But—commanding him to do what?

At least Jupiter knew now that the professor had not been the victim of his own imagination. The mummy really did whisper!

Strapped to his belt, under his coat, Jupe had a portable tape recorder. Modern investigation procedures required scientific equipment, he had said when the boys first started the firm of The Three Investigators. Gradually they had acquired quite a bit of equipment, making or rebuilding most of it from worn-out or junked apparatus that Jupiter's uncle had acquired in the normal operation of The Jones Salvage Yard.

In the little laboratory at Headquarters they had a microscope and apparatus for enlarging fingerprints and making other tests, as well as a darkroom for developing prints of any pictures they took with the flash camera that Bob had contributed. The See-All and the walkie-talkies were new additions Jupiter had made to their equipment that week. The tape recorder was Pete's contribution—he had traded his stamp collection for it with a boy in school.

Now, leaning over the mummy case, Jupiter clipped the small but sensitive microphone of the tape recorder to the linen wrappings only an inch from the mummy's lips.

"I cannot understand you, Ra-Orkon," Jupiter said loudly. "Speak to me again."

At that the whispering, which had momentarily ceased, resumed. A long string of words, uttered in a mere whisper, followed. Jupiter hoped that the sensitive mike could catch the faint sounds.

For more than a minute the whispering continued. Then Jupiter, turning to try to hear better, caught his false beard in a splinter on the edge of the ancient mummy case.

His movement ripped the beard from his chin, and as it came loose, the spirit gum which held it pulled painfully.

"Ouch!" Jupiter said loudly in his own voice. He made a quick grab to get the beard back, lost his balance, and fell heavily. As he fell, his glasses came off and his wig was knocked over his eyes.

Blindly, he stood up and was fumbling to get his disguise back in place when the door burst open and the professor and Bob rushed in.

"What is it, Jupe?" Bob asked.

"We heard you cry out," the professor explained. "Has anything happened?"

"Just my own carelessness," Jupiter said, chagrined. "I'm afraid now I've spoiled everything. The mummy was whispering to me——"

"Then you fooled it!" Bob cried.

"I don't know what I did," Jupe said, sounding cross. "But let me see if it will whisper some more."

He picked up the microphone which had been pulled loose as he fell and had clattered to the floor beside him, and leaned over the mummy case again.

"Speak, Ra-Orkon," he urged. "Speak again."

They all waited, but total silence followed, broken only by their breathing.

"It's no use," Jupiter said at last. "He won't whisper any more. Let's see if the tape recorder caught anything."

He led the way into the next room. Here he removed his disguise and took off the professor's jacket. He placed the portable tape recorder on a desk, rewound the tape and started it over again with the *Play* button depressed.

For a moment there was only the hissing noise of the tape. Then, by listening intently, they were able to hear sounds—words, apparently. The words that the whispering mummy had uttered were muffled by the tape hiss caused by extreme amplification.

"Could you understand it, Professor?" Jupiter asked hopefully when the brief bit of tape came to an end with Jupiter's own "Ouch!" sounding out loudly.

Professor Yarborough, seeming very bewildered, shook his head. "At times I thought I caught a word, but not clearly," he said. "If it is a language of the Middle East, ancient or modern, only one man in California might understand it. He's my old friend, Professor Freeman, whom I mentioned to you earlier." He gestured toward the window through which the home of Professor Freeman was just visible.

"He doesn't live very far away," the professor continued, "but we have to go all around the rim of the canyon to get to him. It will take us only five or ten minutes to reach his home if your chauffeur will drive us there. I propose we go there immediately and let him hear this tape. I have already told him about the mummy whispering to me, and he offered to help if he could, though at the time I don't think he really believed me."

Jupiter agreed that it was a good plan and the professor called Wilkins.

"Wilkins," he said, "the boys and I are going to call on Professor Freeman. You stay and guard the premises. If anything unusual happens, phone me at once."

"Yes, sir," Wilkins agreed.

Inside of five minutes, Bob, Jupiter, and the professor were on their way in the Rolls Royce. By now it was almost dark. After they had gone, Wilkins went to the kitchen, where he had been polishing some Oriental brasswork, and resumed his task. After a short time, a slight noise outside attracted his attention.

It was not repeated, but he rose and, grasping an ancient sword which was part of the professor's collection, he made his way into the museum room. Everything seemed in order. The lid of the mummy case was back in place and the windows were shut, as he had left them after the others had departed.

He opened a window and stepped out onto the terrace. The moment he did so, a voice sounded in his ears. A strange harsh voice seeming to utter some command. Wilkins, his nerves already on edge, stared wildly all around him.

He saw a movement in the shrubbery, and lifted his sword as if to protect himself. A figure moved toward him in the twilight. It was the figure of a man—but it had the head of a jackal, eyes gleaming as they stared at Wilkins.

Wilkins turned deathly pale.

"Annubis!" he choked. "The jackal god!"

Annubis, the dreaded jackal god of Ancient Egypt, took another step toward him, lifted a hand, and pointed it sternly at him.

Wilkins dropped the sword and then, overcome by terror, crumpled beside it in a faint.

Chapter 8

Trapped!

HAVING DRIVEN Professor Yarborough and the two boys to the opposite side of the canyon, Worthington stopped the Rolls Royce in front of the entrance to Professor Freeman's garage. A short bridge connected the garage to the road. The house, built down the slope, was below it.

"Lads, the road is too narrow for me to park here," he said. "Someone might come around that corner too fast and scratch my paintwork."

Worthington was as proud of the old car as if it were his own, and he tended it like a baby.

"There's a parking spot down the road a bit," he said. "A place where the road has been widened so people can stop to see the view. I'll wait for you there."

Climbing out, Yarborough and the boys started down the cement steps which led past the garage to the side of Professor Freeman's home below. When they rang the chime bell, Freeman came to the door.

"This is a pleasant surprise, Yarborough," he said. "Come in, come in. I've just been working on my dictionary of root words of the Middle East. What brings you here?"

When Professor Yarborough explained that he had with him a tape recording of Ra-Orkon actually whispering, Freeman showed great excitement.

"Unbelievable!" he said. "We must play it at once. Let's see if we can understand what the old chap is trying to say."

He led the way into a study crowded with books, record players, and several tape recorders. Swiftly he slid the tape into place on one of the recorders and started it going.

As the harsh whispering of Ra-Orkon, much amplified, filled the room, they all listened intently. But soon Professor Freeman's excitement and expectation changed to perplexity and dismay.

"I'm sorry, Yarborough," he said. "I couldn't make out a word of it. But there's a lot of tape hiss on the recording. Let me get a new noise suppressor I've just received, and try the tape on another machine. Maybe we'll have better luck."

He left the room, returning presently with a small attachment. He placed this and the tape on a second machine and they prepared to listen again.

It was at about the same moment when, on the

other side of the canyon, the light truck from The Jones Salvage Yard pulled up in front of Professor Yarborough's home. It was quite dark now and only a single light shone in the dwelling.

"Looks like nobody home, Pete," Hans, the big Bavarian driver, said as Pete hopped out.

"Wilkins should be here," Pete said. "When I telephoned to the mobile phone in the Rolls Royce, Worthington said he had driven the professor and Bob and Jupe over to a house on the other side of the canyon to consult with someone, but that they would be returning here soon. So I said I'd have you drive me here to meet them. I'll wait and keep Wilkins company until they get back."

"Hokay," Hans said. "I go now. Konrad and me, we want to go to drive-in movie."

Then Hans and the truck were gone. Pete went to the front door and rang. While he waited for an answer, he thought about the case he was handling and what he had learned from his interview with Mrs. Banfry.

Mrs. Banfry had talked a great deal, and very fast, but when you boiled it down, she hadn't really said too much. The gist of it was that her lovely Abyssinian cat, a very rare breed in this country, had been missing for a week. Most Abyssinian cats, Mrs. Banfry said, are wild and unfriendly, but her wonderful Sphinx was different. He was as gentle as a lamb and would go to anyone. She was very much afraid that someone had picked him up and taken him away, or else that he had wandered off and couldn't find his way home again.

She was sure that The Three Investigators, who had done such wonderful work getting back the parrot her friend Miss Waggoner had lost, would find her precious cat.

Pete had had a hard time steering the conversation in the right direction. Finally, though, he had succeeded in getting a description of the cat. It was tawny with white paws, but he couldn't mistake it, Mrs. Banfry told him, because of one very peculiar thing about it—it had mismatched eyes. Most Abyssinian cats had yellow or orange eyes, but Sphinx had one orange eye and one blue eye.

Mismatched eyes in cats, though not common, were not unknown, Mrs. Banfry said. Of course, it meant that Sphinx couldn't win any prizes as a show cat, but on the other hand it gave him the strangest, wisest, most knowing look—as if he understood everything that was being said and could answer if he wanted to.

Sphinx's picture had been in local newspapers and magazines many times because of his eyes, and Mrs. Banfry showed Pete a color picture of the cat that had appeared in a local magazine just six months before. It showed a very nice looking cat with a tawny coat, two white forepaws, and mismatched eyes that gave him a rather eerie appearance.

Pete, having gathered all the information he could, got away as quickly as possible. Now that he had seen Mrs. Banfry, he could rejoin the others. He had finally decided that it was his duty to be with them when they faced the whispering mummy's curse.

He gave up waiting and opened the front door. He entered and called out: "Hello! Wilkins! Where are you? Is anybody here?"

There was no answer. Pete looked around. Nothing seemed wrong. He called out again, then he walked down the passage to the museum room. The door was open and the overhead light on. Everything seemed to be in order, and the mummy case was closed. Near the window the statue of Annubis stood quietly where it was supposed to be.

Nevertheless, Pete had an uneasy feeling that something was not right. He couldn't tell what it was, but a prickly sensation at the base of his spine made him edgy.

He eased slowly into the spooky museum room. He was tempted to open the mummy case and peek in at Ra-Orkon. But he decided against it. Suppose the mummy started whispering to him?

Instead, he crossed to an open French window and looked out. In the dark garden a little glow still lingered in the sky. Not even a breeze stirred. Pete felt that prickly sensation at the base of his spine getting stronger. Darn it, why didn't Jupe and the others get back?

He had just decided to go in, find the telephone, and call Worthington on the mobile phone in the Rolls Royce again when something out on the terrace caught his eye. To see it clearly, he had to step outside. Then he saw that the object on the tiles was a sword. Perplexed, he picked it up. It was a very old sword, made of bronze. He deduced that it was part of the professor's collection. As he held it, a sound behind him made him whirl around.

A movement in the bushes made his heart thump. Then a small animal bounded out and came toward him. It stopped, eased up to him, and rubbed itself against his leg, uttering a loud *purrr* of satisfaction.

"Cat!" Pete laughed aloud at his own alarm. "Just a cat!"

He put down the sword and picked up the cat. It was a large, tawny Tom, and it seemed perfectly friendly. It went on purring as he held it. Then Pete, getting a good look at it, almost dropped it.

It had one orange and one blue eye!

"Gleeps!" Pete exclaimed. "It's Sphinx! Mrs. Banfry's cat! And I've found him right here. I'll certainly have the laugh on Jupe when he gets here and discovers that I've solved the missing cat case all by myself."

He was too tickled by the thought of Jupiter's surprise to wonder at the strange coincidence that made the missing Sphinx turn up at this spot at this moment. Instead, he turned to take the cat into the house.

As he turned, something that felt like a small tiger hit his legs from behind. He went sprawling on the terrace. The cat flew out of his arms and darted off into the bushes.

The next second, Pete was fighting for his life to get away from some small but very active creature that seemd to be all over him.

It took Pete a couple of moments to discover that the creature who had attacked him from behind was a boy. Then he twisted around and got a grip around the other boy's waist and was able to get a look at him.

It was the boy he had tackled in the garden that morning.

Pete was so surprised he almost lost his hold. The boy nearly squirmed free. But Pete got an armhold and twisted him over on the tiles. Then he knelt over the strange boy, holding him down helpless.

"Who are you?" he demanded. "What are you hanging around here for? Why did you tackle me just now?"

The other boy, who had an olive complexion and very black eyes, seemed to be fighting to hold back tears of rage.

"You steal Grandfather Ra-Orkon!" he shouted. "Then you try to steal my cat. But I, Hamid of the House of Hamid, stop you."

Pete blinked in bewilderment.

"What do you mean, I stole Grandfather Ra-

Orkon?" he asked. "And your cat? First place, it isn't your cat, it belongs to Mrs. Banfry. In the second place, I didn't steal it, it came out and wanted to make friends with me."

The boy he was holding down stared at him, scowling fiercely.

"You do not know about Grandfather Ra-Orkon?" he asked. "You did not take him away?"

"I don't know what you're talking about," Pete told him. "If you're talking about the mummy, why do you call him grandfather? He's three thousand years old. And anyway, he's right in there inside in the mummy case."

The other boy shook his head.

"He is gone," he said. "Two men stole him tonight, a little while ago, when no one was here."

"Stole Ra-Orkon!" Pete exclaimed. "I don't believe it."

"Is true," the other boy said. "Hamid of the House of Hamid, from Libya, does not lie."

Pete turned his head to look into the museum room. The mummy case looked undisturbed. But if this boy who called himself Hamid was telling the truth, and the mummy was gone, the whole case had taken a very surprising turn.

"Listen," he said. "All I know is that the mummy was whispering to Professor Yarborough, and we were trying to help him solve the mystery. Maybe you can explain how he came to be whispering?"

The boy he was holding down looked bewildered.

"Grandfather Ra-Orkon whispering?" he asked. "I do not understand. What mystery is this?"

"That's what we're trying to find out," Pete told him emphatically. "You seem to know a lot about the mummy. But maybe I know some things you don't. If you tell me why you were hanging around here this morning and what you want, maybe between us we can solve the mystery."

As Pete spoke, he was thinking that if he could get some more clues to the mystery of the whispering mummy from Hamid, he might be able to wrap up both the mummy case and the case of Mrs. Banfry's missing cat before Jupe and Bob returned. He was human enough to want to get ahead of Jupe just once.

The olive-skinned boy hesitated. Then he nodded.

"Very good," he said. "Hamid of the House of Hamid extends you his trust. Let me up and we will talk."

Pete stood up and dusted himself off. Hamid did likewise. Then he turned and called a series of strange words into the darkness.

"I am calling my cat," he explained. "In it lives the spirit of Ra-Orkon, and it will help us find the mummy."

They waited, but the cat did not come out of the darkness.

"I'm telling you," Pete said, "that cat is Mrs. Banfry's cat, Sphinx. Mismatched eyes, tawny fur, two white forepaws. It fits the description exactly."

"No," said Hamid positively. "Forepaws black, not white. Black like Ra-Orkon's favorite cat, whose mummy was placed with his in the secret burial chamber many centuries ago."

Pete scratched his head. It was true he hadn't taken time to check the forepaws. Maybe he'd made a mistake about the cat. Still, it seemed strange to run into another cat with mismatched eyes the very night he started out to look for a missing cat with that same unusual feature.

"We can settle that later," he said. "Let me see if the mummy is really gone."

He led the way into the museum room. He and Hamid together lifted the lid of the mummy case. What Hamid had said was true. The mummy case was now totally empty.

"He's gone!" Pete exclaimed. "What could have happened to him?"

"You American boys, you had him taken away!" Hamid cried. "You have stolen my grandfather!"

"Now wait a minute, Hamid," Pete said, thinking hard. "I don't know anything about this. Neither do my partners. We were just trying to solve the mystery of why the mummy whispered. You say you don't know about that. Well, as I said, if you tell me what you know and I tell you what I know, maybe we can accomplish something."

The other boy scowled, then nodded.

"Very well. What do you want to know?"

"First, why do you call Ra-Orkon your grandfather? He's three thousand years old."

"Ra-Orkon is ancestor of the House of Hamid," the other boy said proudly. "Three thousand years ago, kings from Libya went to Egypt to rule. Ra-Orkon was a great prince. He was killed because he tried to be just and fair, and was buried very secret to hide him from enemies. His family go back to Libya and today are House of Hamid.

"All this is revealed to my father by the beggar magician, Sardon, who has the gift of tongues and of prophecy and knows the past, the present, and the future. He tells my father that Ra-Orkon is being sent far away to the land of barbarians and will never sleep in peace unless he is brought back and put to rest in proper way.

"My father is ill, so he send Achmed Bey, the manager of his business, as guardian, and me, Hamid, his oldest son, to bring Ra-Orkon back to his home."

Hamid of Libya paused for breath. Another time Pete might have taken exception to being called a barbarian, but just now he thought he was beginning to get the idea. Professor Yarborough had said that some Libyan rug dealer merchant, named Achmed, had tried to persuade him to give up Ra-Orkon. He had sent the fellow off. Unable to make persuasion work, it looked as if Achmed and Hamid had been planning to try to get the mummy in another way.

"So!" he said. "You were hanging around trying to get a chance to steal Ra-Orkon yourself."

"Barbarian professor will not give back my many-times great-grandfather," Hamid said, eyes flashing. "So Achmed and I, we plan to steal him if we can. It is our duty to bring his spirit peace. Achmed disguises himself as a gardener and pays the brothers who take care of this place to let him pretend to be one of them. That way he could always be close. Professor does not notice. As Achmed says, no one looks at gardener. Besides Achmed disguises himself."

"Then it was Achmed, not a real gardener, who grabbed you this morning!" Pete exclaimed. "Your own guardian grabbed you!"

"Yes," Hamid agreed. "He shout to me in Arabic to bite him. I do so and he let me go free. He fool you all. He is very clever, Achmed."

It took Pete a moment to digest this and to comprehend the fact that, all along, the trusted gardener had really been an imposter, a Libyan named Achmed, who wanted to steal Ra-Orkon for Hamid's father. While he was turning it over in his mind, Hamid whirled.

"Someone is outside!" he said. "I heard a truck stop."

He ran to the window that faced on the driveway. Pete joined him. They saw a battered blue truck in the driveway, and two burly men descending from it with the apparent intention of coming straight toward the terrace outside the museum room.

"The same men!" Hamid hissed. "They are the ones who stole Ra-Orkon. I saw them place a wrapped figure in the truck a few minutes ago. And when I saw the house was empty and entered the museum, I found the case but Ra-Orkon was gone."

"They're coming this way," Pete muttered. The men looked like unpleasant customers. "I wonder what they want?"

"We must hide," Hamid said swiftly. "Perhaps they will steal something else. If we hide where we can hear what they say, we may learn where they took Ra-Orkon."

"That sounds good, but where?" Pete looked around. "No place to hide," he said. "Not in here, anyway. Of course if we run outside and hide in the bushes—"

—"Then we cannot hear what is said!" Hamid objected. "Quickly! The mummy case! The case of Ra-Orkon. It is empty. It will hold us. They will never guess someone is in it."

"That's right," Pete agreed. Already the smaller boy had darted across the room to the mummy case and lowered himself into it.

"Swiftly," he called in a whisper. "Come, there is room."

He pressed himself against the side. The men were just outside now. Pete didn't hesitate. He squeezed in beside Hamid. Together they pulled the top of the case back over them. Pete used a pencil stub to hold one corner up so there would be a crack through which they could get air and hear what was said.

They were just in time. An instant after the lid was in place, the door opened and they heard the sound of heavy footsteps.

"You got the strap, Joe?" a voice asked.

"I got it," said a second gruff voice. "Listen, Harry, I'm pretty sore at that customer. Why didn't he say what he wanted in the first place? Making us come back for this old box! I got a good notion to raise the price on him."

"I got the same notion, Joe," the first voice said. "We'll see he pays us—or else. Well, get the strap around it."

An instant later, to the consternation of Pete and Hamid, the mummy case was jostled and one end lifted from the floor. Apparently a strap was being passed around it and pulled tight to hold the lid in place. If Pete had not jammed the pencil in place to leave an air crack, they would have been sealed inside.

"They came back to steal the mummy case, too!" Hamid whispered to Pete in the pitch darkness. "What shall we do?"

"I don't want to tangle with those thugs," Pete whispered back. "We'd better lie low. We have a chance to find out who sent them here in the first place. They'll take us right to him. When he takes the lid off, we'll bust out and start running!"

"Hamid is not afraid," the Libyan boy said stoutly.

"Neither am I," Pete told him. But he certainly felt extremely nervous as the case was lifted and the two men were carrying it outside.

"Dratted thing is mighty heavy," the one called Joe grumbled.

"Like lead," Harry agreed. "Come on, help me heave it into the truck."

The mummy case heaved and tossed. Then it landed heavily inside the truck.

"That'll do it," the deeper voice grunted. "Now let's get going. Wonder what anybody wants with a mummy and an old wooden case, anyway?"

"Some people will collect anything," the other voice said. "Anyway, he's going to have to pay us for making two trips. He's not getting this thing until he does. We'll take it to the hideout and store it until he agrees to pay us extra. Let's go!"

The truck door slammed. A moment later the truck started up the hill, away from Professor Yarborough's home. Tightly strapped inside the case, Hamid and Pete were being taken—where?

Chapter 9

Startling Discoveries

IN THE HOME OF Professor Freeman, Jupiter, Bob, and Professor Yarborough waited while Professor Freeman listened for the twentieth time to the tape of the curious whispering emitted by the mummy of Ra-Orkon.

"I keep feeling I can understand it," he said. "Here and there a word seems to make sense."

He shut off the tape recorder and offered Professor Yarborough a cigar.

"Tell me," he said, "how did you obtain this recording? And, I am most interested to hear about how the statue of Annubis almost fell on you and the ornamental granite ball from the gatepost almost struck you down."

He listened intently while Professor Yarborough told the story. In the middle of it, a doorbell somewhere interrupted him.

"Excuse me, Professor Freeman said, "someone is upstairs at the garage entrance. I'd better see who it is. Make yourselves at home until I return. It's time we took a little break anyway. Then we'll try again."

While Professor Freeman was gone, Professor Yarborough regained his composure.

"I told you that if anyone could understand Ra-Orkon, my old friend Freeman could," he remarked. "His father was my secretary when I discovered the tomb of Ra-Orkon, as I mentioned."

"The one who was murdered just a week after the tomb was opened?" Bob asked.

Professor Yarborough looked distressed.

"Yes," he said. "But please do not attribute his death to a curse of any kind. Aleph Freeman was an adventurous man. I fear he came to harm while exploring Cairo alone by night. However, his son became interested in Egyptology and is now one of the greatest experts on languages of the Middle East."

When Professor Freeman returned, he carried a tray of glasses filled with ginger ale.

"Just a neighbor collecting for some charity," he said. "But as it is so warm, I thought you would like some refreshment. Now let's listen to that tape again while I make notes. I brought along a very rare dictionary from my collection which may help."

Again he played the tape, and again, consulting the dictionary, he jotted down a word here and there. Bob and even Jupe began to wriggle with impatience. At last, Professor Freeman stopped, stretched wearily, went to the window, took a deep breath of air, then turned back.

"I believe I have done all I can," he said. "To be frank, Professor, the message seems to be in a very old form of Arabic in which the words have totally different pronunciation from modern Arabic. However, a certain sense began to emerge. I hesitate to repeat it——"

"Well, go on," Professor Yarborough insisted. "Whatever it is, I want to hear it."

"Well"—Professor Freeman still hesitated—"if I'm right, and remember, I'm only guessing, the gist of the message is: 'Ra-Orkon is far from home. His sleep has been disturbed. Woe to all who disturb his sleep. Peace shall not come to them until peace comes to Ra-Orkon. Nay, they shall join him in death unless Ra-Orkon is restored to his home.' "

Bob Andrews felt a cold chill run down his spine. Even Jupiter turned a little pale. Professor Yarborough looked very unhappy.

"You know I have never put any stock in that so-called curse," he said, sticking his chin out stubbornly. "I refuse to do so now."

"Of course," the other professor agreed. "It would be unscientific."

"Decidedly unscientific," Professor Yarborough stated.

"Still, perhaps I could help," Professor Freeman suggested. "Suppose you brought Ra-Orkon over here for a few days—just to see if he will whisper to me. If we can find out more about this whispering, which I confess puzzles and disturbs me——"

"Just as it puzzles and disturbs me," Professor Yarborough said. "Thank you. But I will not be baffled by a mummy. These boys"—he indicated Bob and Jupiter—"are helping me. Somehow we will get to the bottom of this mystery."

They said good-bye to the younger man and climbed up the stairs to the road above. Worthington was waiting in the big old Rolls Royce in the widened parking space a hundred yards down the narrow road.

"I thought that if anyone could interpret Ra-Orkon's message it would be Freeman," Professor Yarborough remarked as they drove back to his home. "Tell me, Jupiter Jones, have you any theory yet about how Ra-Orkon whispers? Frankly, that interests me much more than any threats or curses."

"No, sir," Jupiter confessed. "So far the case is extremely baffling."

"It's a skull-buster," Bob muttered, using a phrase that was a favorite of Pete Crenshaw's.

"Well, here we are," Worthington said, as he swung the big car down into the space before the professor's home.

"I don't see the truck, but Pete must be here," Jupiter remarked as they all got out. "He phoned Worthington he was going to meet us here."

They went into the house. The lights were on but no one was around.

"Wilkins usually greets me," the professor said,

frowning. He raised his voice. "Wilkins! Wilkins!"

"Pete!" Jupiter also raised his voice. "Are you here?"

Only silence answered them.

"Very strange," the professor said. Jupiter was beginning to look worried.

"Perhaps we should make a search, sir."

"Excellent idea. They may be in the museum."

He led the way down the hall and into the museum room. For a moment they noticed nothing wrong. Then they realized that the mummy case was gone.

"Ra-Orkon!" Bob shouted. "He's gone!"

The professor hastened to the spot where the case had stood. A few slight scratches on the floor were all that remained now. And a crumpled blue bandana handkerchief, which Jupiter pounced on, was on the floor behind a display case.

"Someone has stolen Ra-Orkon!" the professor said incredulously. "Those scratches show where the case was moved. But who would want to steal an ancient Egyptian mummy? It surely has no commercial value."

Then he frowned. "That rug merchant, Achmed Something-or-other," he cried. "He wanted Ra-Orkon! He's the one who did this! I'll have the police on him. Only——" He hesitated and looked about him. "If I call in the police I'll have to tell them about the mummy's whispering. It will be in all the papers. I'll be a laughingstock. I don't think I can afford to call in the police."

He bit his lip, looking unhappy and distracted.

"What shall I do?" he asked. "My scientific reputation is worth more to me than the mummy."

Bob had no suggestion. Jupiter displayed the blue bandana.

"It must have taken at least two men to carry off the case and Ra-Orkon, sir," he said. "So this Achmed, if he had a hand in it, couldn't have done it alone. Bandanas like this are usually carried by workmen. It may be a clue. Perhaps a confederate dropped it. Or it is possible that this Mr. Achmed is innocent and someone else stole Ra-Orkon."

The professor passed his hand across his forehead.

"It's all so confusing," he said. "First the mummy whispers to me—then it vanishes. I really don't know ——" He paused. "Wilkins! We have forgotten all about Wilkins. He was here. I wonder if the scoundrels have harmed him. We must find him."

"You don't suppose he's working with them, do you?" Bob asked. He had read many mysteries in which the butler had turned out to be the criminal.

"Of course not. Wilkins has been with me for ten years! Come help me find him!"

The small white-haired man dashed out on the terrace. His eye caught the sword on the tiles. He picked it up.

"From my collection!" he said. "Wilkins must have seized it to defend himself. They've abducted him, too. Now we must call the police, I'm afraid."

He was about to turn back into the house when a

slight groan reached his ears. It came from behind some bushes just beyond the terrace. Jupiter heard it, too, and he was the first one there.

"It's Wilkins!" he said.

They found Wilkins lying on the grass, his hands crossed upon his chest, hidden behind some shrubs—which was the reason Pete and Hamid had not seen him earlier.

"He was placed here, he didn't fall," the professor said, bending over the butler. "I believe he is about to regain consciousness." He raised his voice. "Wilkins! Can you hear me?"

Wilkins' eyelids quivered, then were still again.

"Look!" Bob exclaimed, catching sight of a small animal in the shadows. "It's a cat!"

"Here, kitty!" He held out his hand. "Here, kitty, kitty!"

The cat, which was licking itself, rose and strolled toward him. Bob picked it up.

"Look," he said, "it has one blue eye and one orange eye. I never saw a cat like that before."

"Good heavens!" Professor Yarborough seemed suddenly agitated. "Mismatched eyes? Let me see!"

Bob held the cat for him to see. Professor Yarborough frowned.

"An Abyssinian cat with mismatched eyes!" he said. "I don't know what to make of this. The whole thing is becoming too—too fantastic. I told you lads that when Ra-Orkon was buried, his favorite royal cat was

the only thing buried with him. Well, that cat was an Abyssinian cat—the royal cat of old Egypt—and it had mismatched eyes and two black forepaws! Look at this cat. It has the same mismatched eyes—and two black forepaws!"

They looked. It was true. The cat had two jet-black forepaws.

"Perhaps Wilkins can tell us something if we can revive him," the professor said. He rubbed the butler's wrists.

"Wilkins, old friend, speak to me," he said. "Tell me what happened!"

The butler opened his eyes. He gazed at Professor Yarborough, but did not seem to see him. His eyes were blank.

"Wilkins. What happened?" the scientist asked. "Who stole Ra-Orkon? Was it that rug merchant?"

Wilkins made an effort to speak.

"Annubis!" he whispered in terror. "Annubis!"

"Annubis?" Professor Yarborough asked. "You're saying that Annubis, the jackal god, stole Ra-Orkon's mummy?"

"Annubis!" Wilkins repeated. Then he closed his eyes again. The professor put his hand on the butler's forehead.

"He has a fever," he said. "Boys, I will have to take him to a hospital at once. I don't believe I'll call the police yet. The newspapers would make a sensational story of it. Wilkins seems to be saying that an ancient

Egyptian god stole Ra-Orkon's mummy. And here we have a cat that looks like the reincarnation of Ra-Orkon's favorite cat of three thousand years ago. I am utterly baffled, but Wilkins' welfare comes first. We'll take him to a hospital in your car if you don't mind. When he can tell us what happened, we will have a better idea of what to do.

"Meanwhile, you take charge of the cat and tomorrow telephone me and we'll see where we stand. Now help me lift Wilkins. We must get him to the car at once."

They got Wilkins into the car and Worthington drove them to a small private hospital run by a friend of the professor's. Wilkins was made comfortable, and soon Bob and Jupiter were on their way back to Headquarters. Bob held the cat, which purred quietly in his arms.

"Golly, Jupe," Bob said. "Do you suppose this cat has anything to do with Ra-Orkon's disappearance?"

Jupiter scowled. "I'm sure it does," he said. "But I haven't the faintest idea what."

Jupe hated to be baffled, Bob knew. And right now he was about as baffled as Bob had ever seen him. He was so baffled that he had even forgotten they hadn't heard from Pete, until Bob spoke.

"Say, where do you think Pete is?" he asked. "We should have heard from him by now."

Jupiter looked startled. "That's right," he said. "We'd better telephone. He may still be at Mrs. Banfry's."

He used the mobile telephone that came with the luxurious car, a telephone from which any number could be called even while the occupant was driving. First he called Mrs. Banfry, who told him that Pete had left a long time ago. Then he called Headquarters and got no answer. Then he called his Uncle Titus, who said that Hans and Konrad had gone to a drive-in movie in the light truck. He also reported, after taking a look, that Pete's bicycle was still parked in the salvage yard.

"Where can he be?" Bob said, looking worried.

"I don't know." Jupe shook his head. "He obviously started for Professor Yarborough's house, but I haven't any idea where he is now. We'll just have to wait until he turns up. I have every confidence in Pete."

His confidence might have been shaken, however, if he had known that at that moment Pete and Hamid, the Libyan boy, tightly strapped inside the mummy case of Ra-Orkon, were being driven toward an unknown destination in downtown Los Angeles.

Chapter 10

No Escape for the Prisoners

THE RIDE INSIDE the mummy case was a long one. The truck bumped over some very bad streets. As Pete and Hamid were squeezed in tightly, however, they were not bounced about too much.

The air began to seem stuffy. Luckily the crack Pete had arranged between the lid and the mummy case was near their faces so they could get some fresh air.

Hamid did not act frightened. Pete had to give him credit for his courage.

"Where do you think they take us?" Hamid asked. He whispered, though whispering was unnecessary. Strapped as they were inside the case in the back of a truck, no one could have heard them even if they had shouted at the top of their lungs.

"From what they said, they're apparently going to hide the mummy case instead of taking it to their customer." Pete said. "When they do that, it will be our chance to escape." He spoke with more assurance than he felt. Suppose the men didn't bother to take the strap off the mummy case before they left it?

"They speak of making two trips," Hamid whispered back. "Of being mad at somebody. What does this mean, Investigator Pete?"

"Someone must have sent them to steal the mummy of Ra-Orkon," Pete said. "They took the mummy, but the case was heavy, so they left it. When they delivered the mummy, whoever sent them was angry at them for not bringing the case. He sent them back for it, and they got mad and decided to hide the case and make him pay extra to get it."

"Ah yes, I think you are right, "Hamid agreed. "But I cannot understand. Who would steal the mummy of Ra-Orkon? He is *my* grandfather, a hundred times away, not someone else's."

"It certainly is a mystery," Pete agreed. "You know, that's probably what Bob Andrews is calling it right this minute, 'The Mystery of the Whispering Mummy.' "

"Bob Andrews?" asked Hamid. "Who is he?"

"He's one of The Three Investigators," Pete said.

"What does that mean?" The younger boy seemed bewildered. Pete started from the beginning and told Hamid all about The Three Investigators. The other boy listened with great interest.

"You American boys, you are so—I cannot think of the word—you go out and do things," he said enviously. "In Libya it is much different. My family buys and sells Oriental rugs. I know much about rugs, but nothing about fingerprints, tape recorders, periscopes, walkie-talkies."

"Walkie-talkie!" Pete exclaimed. "Why didn't I think of it? We can call for help!"

Pete had repaired the walkie-talkie that had been damaged in his struggle with Hamid in the morning. Jupe had instructed the boys that they must have the little radios with them at all times while on a case.

Pete wriggled until he could get the transistorized walkie-talkie out of his pocket. Then he unstrapped the belt antenna from around his waist and poked the end of it through the crack between the lid and the mummy case, feeding the rest of it out inch by inch. When it was all outside, he pressed the *Talk* button.

"Hello, First Investigator!" he said. "This is the Second Investigator calling. Are you reading me? Emergency. Over."

Now he listened. For a moment there was silence. Then his heart leaped. He heard a man's voice.

"Hello, Tom," it said. "Did you hear that? Somebody cut in on us."

"Yeah, Jack," a second voice answered. "Some kid. Listen, kid, whoever you are, shut up. This is business. Now, Jack, like I was saying, my truck is stalled on the Freeway and I got a flat tire. If you'll——"

"Help!" Pete said frantically. "Listen, my name is Pete Crenshaw and I want you to telephone Jupiter Jones in Rocky Beach for me. Extreme emergency."

"Phone who?" the man named Tom asked. "What did you say, kid?"

"Phone Jupiter Jones in Rocky Beach," Pete said urgently. "Tell him Pete needs help badly. Top emergency."

"What kind of emergency, kid?" the man named Jack asked.

"I'm locked in a mummy case. I'm being taken someplace in a truck by the men who stole the mummy of Ra-Orkon!" Pete said. "Jupiter will understand. Please call for me."

"Did you hear that?" the man named Jack laughed. "Some kid says he's locked in a mummy case, and being taken for a ride! These teen-agers! What will they think of next?"

"Please!" Pete yelled. "It's true. Call Jupiter Jones."

"Listen, Tom," the other man said. "You've got my location. Send me some help. You, kid, get lost. Ought to be a law against letting kids jam up the Citizen's Band this way with bad gags."

Then the walkie-talkie went dead. For all of Pete's trying he couldn't get his message through.

"No use, Hamid," he said gloomily. "I should have told those fellows I lost my money or something. When I told the truth about being locked in a mummy case they thought I was a fresh kid trying to jam their conversation."

"It cannot be helped. You tried, Investigator Pete. Is a most unusual happening, to be locked in a mummy case, so they find it hard to believe."

"Yeah, the sort of thing that happens only once

every three thousand years. Then it has to happen to me," Pete grumbled.

They were silent for a while. As the truck rumbled on, Pete started to think of all the things he still wanted to know. If Jupe had been there he would be using the time to good advantage. So Pete started asking questions.

"Listen, Hamid," he said. "How does it happen you speak such good English, if you come from Libya?"

"If I speak English good, I am happy," Hamid said, sounding pleased, although in the total darkness Pete couldn't see his face. "I have American tutor. My father, head of the House of Hamid, wish me to be able to travel all over the world to sell our rugs so I learn English, French, Spanish.

"You see, Investigator Pete, in Libya the House of Hamid has been respected for many, many generations. We make and buy and sell the finest Oriental rugs. But my father is ill. So he has been training me, even though I still am young, to become next head of the House of Hamid."

"Yes, but where does Ra-Orkon come into all this?" Pete asked. "You claim he is your ancestor, but Professor Yarborough says nothing is known about him except his name—nobody knows who he was, what he did—nothing."

"The professor knows only what is in books." Hamid's voice was scornful. "Much knowledge is not in books, and there are wise men who know things that are kept secret from others.

"Six months ago a beggar magician named Sardon came to our home. To my father he said that he had had a vision, and a voice had told him to go to the House of Hamid. My father gave him food, and then the magician Sardon fell into a trance. While in the trance, he spoke in many strange tongues, and then the spirit of Ra-Orkon spoke through his lips.

"Ra-Orkon said that he was soon to be sent to the land of the light-skinned barbarians, and that he could never rest in peace until he returned to his own land. Ra-Orkon said that he was the ancestor of the House of Hamid, and that he called now upon my father to rescue him and give him peace.

"Furthermore, Ra-Orkon said that if my father would go to the land of the barbarians to regain him, he, Ra-Orkon, would appear in the form of his favorite royal cat, the one with eyes that did not match and black forepaws. This would be a sign that he spoke the truth, and thus my father might know it was right and necessary to regain the mummy of Ra-Orkon and return it to Libya.

"After Ra-Orkon had spoken, the beggar, Sardon, awoke and knew nothing of what had been said. He was a very old man, with long white hair, and had but one eye, and limped and walked with a stick. Before he left he looked into a crystal ball with his one eye and told my father many strange things of the past and the future."

—"Golly!" Pete said. "What did your father do then?"

"My father sent Achmed, his manager, to Cairo. Achmed learned that it was true, that in the museum there was the mummy of Ra-Orkon, and it was indeed to be sent far away to the United States,—to a Professor Yarborough in California.

"Achmed reported to my father that Sardon, the beggar, had spoken the truth. So my father, being ill, sent me, his oldest son, with Achmed as my guardian, to this country, to regain the mummy of my many-times great-grandfather. Achmed tried to persuade the professor to give up Ra-Orkon but failed."

"Yes, and the professor sent him away fast," Pete commented.

"That is when Achmed got the plan of pretending to be one of the gardeners, so he could remain close to the mummy and perhaps take it if the chance arose. I, too, remained as close as I could, to help. That is how you happened to catch me this morning. Being strangers in your country, we dare not hurry. We must plan carefully."

"Whiskers!" Pete said, impressed by the tale Hamid had related.

"But why try to steal the mummy? The professor might have sold him to you if you had offered him enough money."

"One does not buy one's own ancestor!" Hamid's voice was icy cold. "The only hope we had was to steal him. We knew that all Sardon had said was true, because one night the spirit of Ra-Orkon mysteriously appeared in my room, as Sardon had said he would, living again in the body of an Abyssinian cat with mismatched eyes and two black forepaws. Ra-Orkon is truly my ancestor, for the words spoken by Sardon have come true. But now"—he paused, sounding bewildered —"someone else has stolen Ra-Orkon. I cannot understand."

Pete's mind was whirling. But one idea came to him.

"Maybe Achmed is the one who hired these thugs, Joe and Harry, to steal Ra-Orkon," he suggested. "Maybe he did it without telling you."

"Is not possible!" exclaimed Hamid. "I would know. He would confide everything to me. I am next head of the House of Hamid."

"Well, maybe," Pete agreed, not feeling too sure Achmed would necessarily tell Hamid everything. Achmed was clever. He might have a plan of his own. "How do you explain Ra-Orkon starting to whisper?"

"I do not know. Perhaps Ra-Orkon is angry. Perhaps he is angry with me and Achmed, and with the professor, too, It is all a great mystery to me." In the total darkness inside the mummy case, Hamid sounded very troubled.

"I'll buy a triple helping of that," Pete said. "Hey, we seem to be stopping."

The truck had, indeed, stopped. They heard something that sounded like a garage or warehouse door, sliding up. The truck moved a few feet and stopped again. They heard the door being lowered, and knew they were inside a warehouse or storeroom or garage.

The rear of the truck was opened. A moment later the mummy case was being lifted out, not gently. Both Pete and Hamid were badly jostled as the two men carried the case a few feet and let it fall with a thud to the floor.

"Come on, Joe," said Harry's voice. "Nobody will bother it here."

"Right," Joe answered. "We'll phone the customer in the morning and tell him we want the price doubled. He can worry tonight."

"Tomorrow we're busy," the other said. "You forget that job we promised to do in Long Beach?"

"That's right. Okay, let him worry all day tomorrow. By evening he'll be in a real sweat. Then we'll phone him and tell him we'll make delivery if he'll pay the price."

"Maybe we'll triple it," Harry suggested. "He was certainly anxious to get the case to go along with the mummy. Okay, let's get going."

The door opened again. The truck motor roared to life and the boys heard the truck begin to back out.

With fast-beating hearts, they pushed against the lid of the mummy case.

They pushed in vain. It would not budge for them. Joe and Harry had left it strapped tightly shut.

Chapter 11

Bob and Jupiter are Worried

BOB ANDREWS sat at the typewriter in Headquarters, typing up his notes. He knew how to type because his father, a writer for a Los Angeles newspaper, had enrolled him in a typing course when he was twelve.

Jupiter Jones was sitting with the strange cat which had appeared at Professor Yarborough's home in his lap. It was purring loudly while he stroked it with one hand. With the other hand he was pinching his lips, always a sign his mental machinery was in overdrive.

"Golly," Bob said, "it's five minutes to ten. Pete still hasn't shown up. What could have happened to him?"

"Perhaps Pete is following some clue," Jupiter suggested.

"He's supposed to be home by ten o'clock," Bob said. "So am I. In fact, I have to leave pretty soon or my folks will be worrying."

"Perhaps if you phone they'll let you stay here a little longer," Jupiter said. "In the meantime, maybe Pete will show up."

Bob used the office telephone, for which they paid by helping Mr. Titus Jones rebuild usable junk that came into the salvage yard. When he resold it, he gave them half the profits.

Bob's mother answered, and upon hearing that he was with Jupiter Jones, agreed to let him stay an extra half hour.

Now Jupiter put down the purring cat. He used the See-All to survey the outside territory, partially lit by the salvage yard entrance light and a street lamp. All was quiet. In the small cottage beyond the yard, where he lived with his uncle and aunt, a light in the living room indicated that they were watching television. A smaller cottage behind it was dark. This was where Hans and Konrad, the husky yard helpers, lived. Jupiter would have liked to ask Hans where he had last seen Pete, but he knew Hans was at a drive-in movie with his brother.

Jupiter swiveled the periscope and saw a car coming down the street. It slowed, then speeded up again. Under the street light he could see it was a flashy, blue sports car. There was a tall, thin youth behind the wheel.

Jupiter returned to the desk.

"No sign of Pete," he said. "But Skinny Norris just drove by."

"He did?" Bob exclaimed. "Now what's he up to?"

"Probably curiosity," Jupiter stated. "He's wondering what we're up to. He has probably figured out we have a case on and wants to horn in somehow."

"He'll get a punch in the nose if he isn't careful!" Bob exclaimed. "He's a born snoop."

Skinny Norris was a tall, thin, long-nosed boy, slightly older than the others, whose chief ambition was to prove himself smarter than Jupe. So far his efforts had resulted in failure, but that made him even more willing to go to any lengths to get the better of Jupiter and Bob and Pete.

Jupiter, however, was no longer thinking about Skinny Norris. He was more worried about Pete's absence than he showed. He was beginning to think that perhaps he had encountered a mystery that was too big for The Three Investigators, and that he might have to call for help from the authorities. Being somewhat stubborn, he hated to admit he was at a loss. Besides, Professor Yarborough was anxious to avoid any publicity. He weighed all the various factors and made a decision.

"We'll give Pete another half hour to show up," he said. "Then we'll take action."

Bob stopped typing. His mind was a whirling merry-go-round of strange events—a whispering mummy that had vanished, a falling statue, a runaway granite ball, a cat with mismatched eyes, an ancient Egyptian curse. He couldn't think straight any longer.

"Jupe," he said, "I better get on home. I'm bushed."

Jupiter nodded. "We can all use a good night's sleep," he said. "But I'll wait awhile in the hope that

Pete will show up or phone."

"Why don't you give the walkie-talkie a try?" Bob suggested. "Pete might be trying to contact us that way."

"I should have given them greater range when I built them," Jupe grumbled. "When I rebuild them, I will tend to that. However, let's see."

He pressed the button on the small loudspeaker that doubled as a walkie-talkie unit.

"Headquarters calling the Second Investigator," he said. "Come in, Second. Come in if you read me."

The speaker hummed but no answer came.

"He's not broadcasting now," Jupiter said. "Or else he's out of range. I'll stay here by the set. You go on home."

Reluctantly Bob pedaled home. He was lost in such deep thought as he entered the house that his father, who was home early—he worked evenings on a big morning newspaper—had to speak twice to get his attention.

"Why the deep thought, Bob?" his father asked. "School is out so it can't be an examination."

"It's a case." Bob perched on the arm of his father's chair. "It's kind of mysterious."

"Want to tell me about it?"

"Well, it partly involves a cat with one blue eye and one orange eye," Bob said, to which his father answered, "Hmmm," and reloaded his pipe.

"But mostly it's about a mummy that whispers. How

can a 3,000-year-old mummy whisper actual words?"

"That one's easy." His father chuckled. "The same way a wooden dummy can be made to talk."

"What's that, Dad?" Bob asked with eager interest.

"Ventriloquism," his father said and lit his pipe. "Let's go at this logically. A mummy can't talk or whisper. Therefore someone else must make it seem to whisper. The way to do this is by ventriloquism. Conclusion: if you have a 3000-year-old mummy that is whispering, look for a ventriloquist somewhere in the neighborhood."

"Golly, Dad," Bob said, "that could be the answer. Excuse me while I phone Jupe."

"Surely," his father said and smiled as Bob went out to the hall to the telephone. He remembered himself as a boy and some of the strange things he'd been interested in, which made him more sympathetic with Bob's activities than he might otherwise have been.

Bob rapidly dialed the number at Headquarters. When Jupiter answered, he sounded disappointed.

"I hoped it was Pete," he said. "What do you have to report, Bob?"

"I was discussing the case with my father," Bob told him. "He said one way to make a mummy whisper is to use ventriloquism. He suggested that we look for a ventriloquist in the neighborhood."

"I thought of that," Jupiter informed him. "But a ventriloquist working from a distance would have to use a small radio. We proved there wasn't any radio.

And when I went in disguised as Professor Yarborough, the mummy whispered to me. We both know I wasn't doing any ventriloquism, so that hardly seems the answer."

"Well, think about it anyway," Bob said. "Maybe someone could have been hiding just outside the door and casting his voice inside. Say, have you called the professor's house to see if Pete is there?"

"I shall do so at once," Jupiter answered. "Meanwhile, I will give more thought to the possibility of ventriloquism. It seems impossible, but Sherlock Holmes once said that when you have ruled out all other answers, what remains must be true."

He and Bob hung up. Bob went to bed, worried about Pete, but unable to think of anything to do. Jupiter dialed Professor Yarborough's house, but there was no answer—the professor was apparently still at the hospital with the butler.

Even as Jupiter telephoned, Pete and Hamid were shoving with all their might against the lid of the mummy case, trying to push their way out.

But as they strained, they heard a sound which caused them to pause. The truck was coming back. They heard the door slide up again.

Then they heard the truck stop, and the two men got out.

"Good idea to cover this thing up," one of the men said. "Nobody but us is supposed to come in here, but in case anyone does, no use getting them curious."

The two boys heard a rustling sound as a heavy canvas was draped over the mummy case.

"It'll cut off our air!" Pete whispered to Hamid. "I'm going to yell for help. We can't stay cooped up in here."

He drew in a deep breath to yell. Then, at the next words of the men outside, he held it and did not utter a sound.

Chapter 12

A Wild Flight

"LISTEN, JOE," the man named Harry said. "We may need the canvas strap tomorrow."

"You're right," Joe answered. "Let's take it."

Pete and Hamid waited tensely. They heard the canvas being dragged off. Then the mummy case rocked as the men loosened and pulled free the canvas strap that made a prison out of it. A moment later, the canvas was replaced and they heard the truck motor start up. The truck backed out and the big door closed.

An instant later Pete and Hamid were both thrusting upward. Now the lid of the mummy case came off without difficulty. They scrambled out and crawled from under the heavy tarpaulin.

Because of the darkness, they couldn't see too much. But a little light came in through a skylight in the ceiling from street lamps outside. This enabled them to see that they were in a storeroom that had high ceilings and solid concrete walls without any windows.

They began to explore. First they discovered that a

truck-sized metal door gave entrance into the room, but that it was securely locked from the outside. They could rattle it slightly, but that was all.

Then in the semi-darkness they examined the contents of the storeroom. They found an odd conglomeration of objects in it. First to attract their notice was an old automobile. Partly by feel and partly by the faint light, they figured that it was an ancient Pierce-Arrow sedan, very old and elegant.

"An old automobile," Hamid said wonderingly. "Why should such a thing be here?"

"It's an antique. Probably goes back to about 1920. Cars like this are very valuable to collectors," Pete told him.

The next objects they came to were many pieces of furniture. These were heavy and intricately carved, as they could tell by running their fingers over them. All were set on a raised wooden platform.

"To keep them dry," Pete said. "They're being stored. But what's this? A big pile of something here."

Hamid excitedly touched a mound made up of a dozen long, thick cylinders stacked in a pyramid.

"Rugs!" he said. "Oriental rugs. Fine ones. Most valuable!"

"How can you tell that in the dark?" Pete asked. "I can see they're rugs, but that's all."

"My fingers tell me. When I am eight years old my father teach me to know a rug from any place in Orient by touch. It is a matter of weave, and kind of wool, and many little things. None of these is from the House of Hamid, but all are most valuable. Two thousand, three thousand dollars each!"

"Golly, they may have been stolen," Pete said. "I'll bet everything in this storeroom has been stolen and that those two men, Joe and Harry, are professional thieves. That's probably why they were hired to steal Ra-Orkon and his mummy case."

"It is so," Hamid agreed. "I feel you are correct. But how shall we now get out of this place?"

"Here's a door," Pete said, finding a small door almost lost in the darkness. It was set into a solid brick wall that seemed to cut this storeroom off from the rest of the building.

He grabbed the knob of the door and turned. The door would not budge. Then they spotted another door. But this just led to a small washroom.

"My guess is," Pete said at last, "that this space back here is a secret hideout for stolen goods, and no one can get into it but Joe and Harry. There's still one way out, though."

"What is that?" Hamid asked. "I see no way. Just strong walls without openings."

"Up there," Pete pointed. Hamid looked up. The single skylight that let some outside light into the storeroom was open a few inches. But it was a dozen feet above their heads.

"If we could but fly," Hamid said, "we could emerge that way."

"Let's see what we can do," Pete told him. "Look at the old car. It's standing almost under the skylight."

"That is true," Hamid agreed eagerly. "Quickly, let us see if it gives us enough height."

"Take it easy, Hamid," Pete cautioned the smaller boy as Hamid was about to climb up on top of the grand old vintage Pierce-Arrow limousine. "Your shoes will scratch the paint. That will damage a car that's practically a museum piece."

Both boys removed their shoes so they would not damage the paint of the fine old car, and with the laces tied together and the shoes slung around their necks, they climbed on top of the car. But even when Pete stretched to his full height, the skylight was a foot above him and more than a foot beyond the car.

"I'm going to jump for it, Hamid!" Pete said. "We can't stay here!"

He leaped. His fingers caught the metal edge of the open skylight. It took a moment to push the skylight wide open, then he pulled himself up and wriggled out onto a gravel-covered roof. Immediately he leaned down inside the skylight and stretched out his hands.

"Jump, Hamid, I'll catch you," he said. "Grab for my wrists."

For a moment the smaller boy hesitated. He looked down at the concrete floor. Then resolutely he looked up at Pete, stretched his arms, and jumped.

His fingers barely caught Pete's wrists. Pete wrapped his own hands around Hamid's slender wrists and heaved. A moment later Hamid was beside him on the roof.

"You are very strong, as well as brave, Investigator Pete," Hamid said admiringly.

The praise made Pete feel good.

"Do tougher things than that every day in gym," he said, in an offhand manner. "Now let's put our shoes on and see how we get off this roof."

At the front, the roof ran into a high brick wall, where the front of the building rose. They could not go that way. But at the rear there was an iron ladder for access to the roof for repairs and painting. It took them only a moment to climb down to the dark alley beneath. Here they paused to figure out where they were.

As they looked around, Pete took a piece of blue chalk from his pocket and chalked several large question marks on the lower left-hand corner of the truck entrance door to the storeroom.

"That's our special mark," he explained to Hamid. "It'll help us find this spot where the mummy case is hidden when we come back for it. Now let's go down the alley to the street and get the address of this building and—oh–oh, someone coming. Maybe a tramp or a criminal. Better go the other direction to the street behind us."

They hurried down the long alley, between the dark, silent, closed back doors of shops, and emerged on a poorly lit, run-down street. Pete did not recognize anything about it, and knew he had never been in this part of town before.

"We've got to know where we are," he told Hamid. "Come on—down to the next corner. We'll see the name of the street there and make a note of it so we can find our way back here."

But at the next corner the street sign under a dirty street light was badly bent and damaged so they could not read it. Someone must have thrown rocks at it, ruining it.

"Darn!" Pete said. "Some people——"

At that moment somewhere down the side street came a sound of smashing glass. Then two men ran past them and jumped into a car that roared away.

Pete and Hamid stared after them, and were startled to hear an angry bellow behind them.

"Stop, thief!" a man roared. "You boys! You smashed my store window! You stole my watches! Wait'll I get you!"

A big man was running toward them, shaking his fist. He obviously believed they were guilty of the crime that had just been perpetrated.

Pete obeyed his first instinct, grabbed Hamid's hand, and said, "Run!"

They ran. Up one street, down another, and through alleys. Other people joined their pursuer, and a couple of dogs, too. They ran until they were breathless and had lost all sense of direction before they lost their last pursuer and stopped.

"Maybe we should have tried to tell that man that we didn't smash his window," Pete said, gasping for breath. "The truth is, I just ran before I thought about it."

"When someone cries 'Thief!' and runs at you, to flee is the natural thing," Hamid said. "You must not blame yourself."

"But the trouble is," Pete said, scowling, "I don't know where we were when we started running. It was blocks away, that's all I know. Do you realize we haven't the faintest idea where that storehouse is."

"Is true," Hamid said soberly. "Is another problem, is it not, Investigator Pete?"

"It sure is," Pete said. "How're we going to find it again? And how're we going to get home? We must be fifteen miles away from Rocky Beach and ten miles from Hollywood, anyway. We're someplace in downtown Los Angeles."

"We take a taxi cabin," Hamid said.

"Taxi cab," Pete told him. "That needs money."

"Oh, I have money," Hamid assured him. "Achmed gives me money for emergency. I have many U.S. dollars."

He showed Pete a wallet stuffed with dollar bills.

"Fine," Pete said. "There are some bright lights. Maybe down that way we'll find a cab."

They hurried down the street. At the corner they found a taxi stand and a driver who readily consented to make the long trip to their homes when Hamid showed him that they had money to pay for the ride.

Before starting their ride, Pete made a note of the location. At least it was within fifteen or twenty blocks of the secret storehouse where Ra-Orkon's case now reposed. And he used an outdoor pay phone to give Jupiter a quick call.

"I'm okay," he said. "I'm starting home. Too much to tell you now. I'll call as soon as I get home."

"Use the walkie-talkie," Jupe said. "I'll be in my room waiting. I'm glad to hear from you, Second."

Jupe sounded so relieved that Pete knew he had been genuinely worried. But wait until Jupe learned he had been right at the spot where the mummy case had been taken—and had lost it!

Pete hopped into the cab with Hamid and they started back. The ride was without incident. Hamid insisted that Pete go home first. Then, he said, he would ride back in the taxi to the house Achmed had rented for them near Professor Yarborough's house.

When they reached Pete's home in Rocky Beach, Hamid stopped Pete as he was about to leave the cab.

"Investigator Pete," he said, "will you and your friends help to find the mummy of Ra-Orkon and the mummy case? I, Hamid of the House of Hamid, wish to engage your services."

"Well," Pete said, "the mummy really belongs to Professor Yarborough, and we're already working for him."

"Work for Hamid, too," the boy urged. "Just to find

Ra-Orkon and the mummy case. Return them to the professor. Then Achmed and I will try again to persuade the professor to give them up."

"I guess we can do that," Pete said. "All right, you'll need to talk to Jupe. Be at the Jones Salvage Yard at about ten tomorrow morning."

Hamid agreed. They shook hands and Pete hurried into his home, aware that he was very late. His father and mother were watching television. His father, a powerfully built man, was a special effects man for one of the Hollywood movie studios.

"You're late, Pete," he said. "Your mother and I were worried."

"Yes, sir," Pete said. "You see I started out to hunt for a missing cat and I sort of—well, I got a bit sidetracked."

He was about to tell the whole story, but his mother shook her head.

"You go take a bath, son, and get into bed," she said. "Gracious, how do boys get so dirty?"

"Yes, Mom," Pete agreed and trudged up the stairs.

He hurried to his room, opened the window, let the belt antenna dangle out, and pressed the *Talk* button of his walkie-talkie.

"Second Investigator calling Headquarters," he said. "Second Investigator calling Headquarters. Can you read me? Come in, Headquarters."

He let up on the button and waited. Almost at once Jupe's voice replied.

"This is First Investigator," he said. "I'm in bed, but I've kept tuned in. Are you all right? What happened?"

Giving just the bare essentials, Pete supplied him with a swift account of the evening's happenings, ending with the fact that he did not know where he and Hamid and the mummy case had been taken.

Jupe was silent for a moment.

Then, "You cannot be blamed, Second," he said. "You did very well, and we will somehow locate the mummy case. In the morning we must all have a conference. Several new facts have emerged. All of them make the mystery seem darker. For one thing, I have here the cat you mentioned, the cat the boy Hamid claims is the reincarnation of Ra-Orkon. However, it is not.

"I am quite sure from what you tell me that the cat with the mismatched eyes is really Mrs. Banfry's cat in disguise."

With that Jupe signed off, leaving Pete to go to bed to toss and turn with a new curiosity.

How could a cat be in disguise?

Chapter 13

Jupiter Has Suspicions

THE FOLLOWING MORNING, The Three Investigators met for a conference in Headquarters. Pete and Bob could tell by Jupiter's expression that he had done a lot of thinking since the previous night. But he was in no hurry to satisfy their curiosity about his new ideas.

"I do not like to guess," he said. "First we must have our conference, and we cannot begin until the boy Hamid is here."

Pete, using the See-All, spotted a taxi coming into the salvage yard and saw Hamid get out. He hurried out through Tunnel Two to get Hamid and bring him back through the tunnel. As Hamid was a client, and would in any case soon be going home to Libya, they didn't mind letting him know about the hidden Head-quarters.

"Hamid," Pete said, "this is Bob Andrews, in charge of records and research, and this is First Investigator Jupiter Jones."

"I am most pleased to meet Bob and First Investigator Jupiter," the small Libyan boy said in formal English.

"Now," Jupiter said, "I'd like a complete story of everything that happened to you last night, Pete, from the time you left us. Bob, take notes."

Pete embarked upon the story of his interview with Mrs. Banfry about the missing Sphinx, then his arrival at Professor Yarborough's house, and all the rest of the adventurous events of the evening. Bob, who had studied shorthand while he was learning typing, was kept busy getting it all down. Much of it was new to him. The facts about the mummy case being stolen, and Pete and Hamid's ride in it, he was hearing for the first time."

"Golly," he said, when Pete had finished. "You mean you actually were in the storeroom where those thieves hid the mummy case? And you don't even know the address?"

"I tell you we were running like anything," Pete said. "We were too busy to stop and read any street signs. I know the general neighborhood within about twenty blocks."

"Twenty blocks!" Bob exclaimed. "That's four hundred blocks of streets to search, if you take an area twenty blocks on each side. And if only half the streets are connected by alleys——"

"Remember, Pete marked the door of the storeroom with our secret mark," Jupiter interrupted. "When we find the question marks, we will know we have the right place."

"But we have only until tonight!" Bob yelped. "And to search all those alleys——"

"I have a plan," Jupiter said. "But it will take time. For the moment, let us consider the strange mystery of the mummy that whispered to Professor Yarborough."

"The mummy of Ra-Orkon, the ancestor of the House of Hamid!" Hamid cried. "Do you know how you can find him?"

Jupiter pinched his lip. "Not yet," he said. "But I must make a correction, Hamid. I do not think Ra-Orkon is an ancestor of your family."

Hamid looked angry. Then he looked bewildered.

"But Sardon said he was," he stated stubbornly. "And Sardon was a magician. He had the gift of tongues and prophecy. He went into a trance and spirits spoke to him. He was a man of great power, and my father knew that he spoke truth. So I know also."

"It is true," Jupiter said, "that kings from Libya took over the leadership of Egypt during the 20th Dynasty, about three thousand years ago."

"And Ra-Orkon was Libyan prince," Hamid said stubbornly. "Sardon said so."

"Perhaps he was," Jupiter admitted. "Even Professor Yarborough is not sure who Ra-Orkon was, or when he was buried. He could have been a Libyan prince. But that doesn't necessarily make him your ancestor, Hamid."

"Sardon said so!" Hamid had become very stubborn

now. "Sardon, the magician, spoke truth."

"Not entirely," Jupiter said. "He was wrong about the cat. And if he didn't tell the truth about one thing, he may not have told the truth about everything."

"I do not understand," Hamid scowled.

"Well," Jupiter said, "according to your story, this magician, Sardon, said that after you got here to America, the spirit of Ra-Orkon, reincarnated in the shape of his favorite cat, an Abyssinian cat with mismatched eyes and black forepaws, would appear to you as a sign that his words were true."

"That is so," Hamid answered stoutly. "And it happened. The spirit of Ra-Orkon, as a cat, appeared mysteriously in my room one night last week."

"That's just it——" Jupiter began, but here Pete put in a word.

"What's this reincarnation mean?" he asked. "I sort of think I know but I'm not sure."

"In the Orient," Jupiter told him, "many truly religious people believe that after they die they are born again, sometimes in the shape of a lower animal or even an insect. This is called reincarnation."

"Yes," Bob put in. "And sooner or later they get reborn as human beings again."

"And Ra-Orkon's spirit was reborn as an Abyssinian cat, exactly matching his favorite cat who was buried with him," Hamid said. "As you say, First Investigator Jupiter, it has mismatched eyes and black forepaws."

"That's just it," Jupiter said. "I want to show you

something—something important."

He disappeared into the small adjoining laboratory and came back with a cat purring in his arms.

"Ra-Orkon!" Hamid cried. "Honored ancestor, I am happy you are safe."

"He appeared last night out of the bushes at Professor Yarborough's house," Jupiter said. "I brought him home to take care of him. But now I want you to watch carefully."

Jupiter took out a handkerchief and wet it with some cleaning solvent. Then he rubbed one of the cat's black forepaws. The handkerchief took on a black streak and the black forepaw turned white.

"The cat really has white forepaws," he told Hamid. "See? It's actually Mrs. Banfry's cat, Sphinx, with its forepaws dyed black to look like the cat Sardon predicted would appear to you."

Now Pete understood what Jupiter had meant when he said that the cat was in diguise.

"Golly," he exclaimed, "why would anyone want to disguise a cat?"

Little Hamid reached out for the cat. He studied the white forepaw which had been black a moment earlier.

"Is true!" he cried. "Cat has been disguised. It is not Ra-Orkon's spirit. The magician beggar, Sardon, said positively that the cat that would appear would have black forepaws like the cat of Ra-Orkon."

"Which means," Jupiter said, taking his seat again, "that Mrs. Banfry's cat, Sphinx, has been disguised for the purpose of making you believe that the beggar's prophecy was coming true."

"But why?" Hamid asked, and Pete echoed the word. "Why?" he asked.

"So that Hamid's father and Achmed would believe the rest of the story, too, about Ra-Orkon being an ancestor, and would try to get the mummy of Ra-Orkon back from the professor," Jupiter said. "I'm pretty sure the truth is, Hamid, that Ra-Orkon is not your ancestor at all."

"Ra-Orkon *is* our ancestor!" Hamid's dark eyes flashed. He seemed close to tears and was fighting them back. Jupiter changed the subject.

"The truth will come to light when we find out who stole Ra-Orkon, and why," he said tactfully. "Pete has told his part of the story. Now, Hamid, suppose you tell us everything you told Pete last night, so Bob can take notes."

Hamid gladly obliged. He told about the arrival at his home in Libya of the lame, half-blind, wandering magician, Sardon. He told about Sardon's trance in which the spirit of Ra-Orkon spoke through his lips, begging Hamid's father to rescue him from the land of the barbarians.

He told how he and Achmed had come to America and rented a house near Professor Yarborough's. Then he told how, after Achmed had asked the professor to return Ra-Orkon, and had been refused, Achmed had paid the Magasay brothers to let him serve as the professor's gardener. That way he could always be near the mummy, alert for a chance to obtain it.

"Golly," Bob exclaimed at that point. "So it was Achmed hanging around the house all the time! It was Achmed who grabbed you when Pete spotted you. No wonder you were able to get away!"

"Achmed tells me to bite his hand, and I do," Hamid said proudly. "Achmed is very clever."

"Tell me, Hamid," Jupiter asked, "did you and Achmed know about the supposed curse on the mummy?"

"Surely," the Libyan boy answered. "Sardon told us about it. He said that Ra-Orkon, could not rest easily until we gave him peace."

"Certain mysterious events occurred," Jupiter went on. "The statue of Annubis toppled over. A mask fell off the wall. My deduction is that Achmed caused these occurrences."

"Yes." Hamid showed white teeth in a grin. "As gardener in overalls nobody noticed him. He stood outside tall windows. With a long rod he pushes through crack between window and wall and made Annubis fall over. Then he pushed mask off wall. Also he picked mortar from around stone so it would roll off. He tried to scare professor into giving up Ra-Orkon."

"As I thought," Jupiter said. "That's how easily an old Egyptian curse can be made to work. With the help of a gardener who seems trustworthy but is really an adversary in disguise."

"Well, okay," Pete said. "But how do you explain Ra-Orkon being stolen? Hamid swears Achmed had nothing to do with that. And who stole Mrs. Banfry's cat? And why was it disguised and slipped into Hamid's room? Those are still pretty mysterious mysteries, it seems to me."

"Yes," Bob chimed in. "And we haven't mentioned the mummy's whispering to the professor, which Hamid didn't even know about. How do you explain that?"

"One thing at a time," Jupiter said, his manner lofty. "Hamid, did you actually see those two men, Joe and Harry, steal Ra-Orkon?"

"Yes." Hamid nodded. "Last night Achmed says his hand hurts him and he wishes to rest. So when it gets dark I slip down road to watch professor's house. Cat follows me. I am just in time to see two men carry Ra-Orkon wrapped in cloth out of house, put him into truck."

"That was after we had all gone over to Professor Freeman's," Bob remarked.

"I wait, not knowing what to do," Hamid went on. "Then Investigator Pete arrives. I wait some more in bushes. He walks around in house, then out on terrace, and takes my cat. I decide it is he and you who have had Ra-Orkon stolen and are now stealing cat. I get very angry and attack him. I am sorry, Investigator Pete."

"No harm done," Pete said. "In fact, that was what

helped us to get together and join forces on this mystery."

"Mmm." Jupiter was pinching his lip, looking thoughtful. "So far the picture, though complicated, is clear."

"That statement," Pete declared, "is complicated and unclear. To me the mystery is more of a skull-buster than ever."

"I mean," Jupiter said, "we seem to have all the facts. Now we must make some sense of them."

Bob only wished he could make some sense of all the facts he had written down. The more he thought about them, the more his mind whirled helplessly.

"I believe," Jupiter said, "that if we can find the hiding place of the mummy case, we will be on the road to solving the mystery. I propose that we locate the hidden storeroom, then wait. No doubt sometime tonight Harry and Joe will deliver the mummy case to this mysterious customer, who already has the stolen mummy. By following them we will catch the customer, who is the master criminal behind the whole scheme, and get the mummy back."

It was obvious Jupiter was rather pleased with the idea of catching someone who could be called a master criminal.

"Then," he said, "we will have the criminal, the mummy, and the mummy case. When that is done, the answers to the other mysteries will soon follow."

"Great," Pete said with heavy sarcasm. "Just great.

Well, with all those alleys to search for the secret symbols I chalked, we'd better be going. It may take us a week or two and we have only eight or nine hours."

"That is not my plan," Jupiter said. "Instead, early this morning I took certain steps. You remember the Ghost-to-Ghost Hookup we used in the stuttering parrot case?"

They did indeed. It was a brainstorm of Jupe's which had enabled them to solve the case.

But Hamid looked puzzled. "Please, what is that— Ghost-to-Ghost Hookup?"

"A Ghost-to-Ghost Hookup," Jupiter explained, "involves calling several boys for information, and asking each of them to call several others, who in turn will call others, until hundreds or even thousands of boys all over Los Angeles are trying to learn something The Three Investigators need to know. Anyone who learns the needed facts calls us back at Headquarters. Then we are able to proceed with the new knowledge. In the stuttering parrot case the Ghost-to-Ghost Hookup turned up a boy named Carlos, whose uncle had sold the mysterious parrots which were the central clues to that exciting case."

Hamid listened with great interest.

"Well," Jupe said, "this morning I called five boys whose fathers work in downtown Los Angeles. I asked them to call other friends whose fathers also worked in downtown Los Angeles. Each boy was to ask his father to look for blue question marks chalked on a storeroom door, and if he saw any, to note the address for his son. As an explanation, I said it was a sort of treasure hunt. And the first boy who called in the information we needed would get a reward. I'll worry about what that will be, later. Now, let us see if my plan is being carried out."

He picked up the telephone and called. He spoke to a friend briefly, holding the phone so they could all hear the conversation over the small microphone and radio speaker he had rigged up—the same speaker which he now used as the Headquarters unit for their walkie-talkies.

The boy reported that he had phoned five friends as requested, and they had all asked their fathers to be on the lookout for chalked blue question marks. Of course, none of them would know if any question marks had been seen until the men returned home from work, around six that evening.

"The Ghost-to-Ghost Hookup is in effect," Jupe said said as he hung up. "Unfortunately, we can't hope for information before evening. Our time will be short but if we have luck, we will be able to go straight to the spot. Right now I'd like to drive out to have another talk with Professor Yarborough."

"But your aunt won't let you get away," Pete reminded him. "I heard her say you had to pitch in and work as soon as our conference is over."

"Mmm. That's true." Jupiter nodded. "I'll phone him instead. Meanwhile, Bob, you show Hamid the way out and call a taxi for him."

"Sure thing," Bob said.

Hamid rose. "Some time I wish Achmed to meet you, First Investigator Jupiter," he said. "He thinks all American boys are loud and have bad manners and annoy their elders. I will show him some American boys are very clever indeed."

"Thank you, Hamid," Jupiter said, visibly pleased with the words. "By the way, you haven't told Achmed all that has happened, have you?"

"I have said only that I have engaged you to help find Ra-Orkon and the mummy case," Hamid told him. "He snorted at that, and said it was foolish to ask children to do a man's work, so I told him nothing more."

"That's good," Jupiter said. "I mean it's good that you didn't tell him anything else. I've noticed that adults can't help trying to be helpful when they learn a boy is engaged upon some important project, and often they spoil everything. In this case, secrecy is very important, for neither Professor Yarborough nor the House of Hamid wishes any publicity."

"That is true," Hamid said. "When shall we meet again?"

"Come back this evening at about six," Jupiter said. "By then if we're lucky we'll have some word from our Ghost-to-Ghost Hookup giving us the location of the storeroom where the mummy case is hidden."

"I will be back," Hamid said. "I will come by taxi.

Achmed is very busy today. He says he has many rug buyers to see."

He made a little formal bow and followed Bob down into Tunnel Two and out of Headquarters.

"Hamid's a nice little guy," Pete said, when the other two boys had gone. "But I've been watching your face, Jupe, and you've had a new idea just since we started talking. You think you know now who stole Ra-Orkon, don't you?"

"I have a suspicion," Jupiter said. "You told me that Mrs. Banfry's cat, Sphinx, had been written up in several magazines and papers, with pictures of its mismatched eyes."

"That's right," Pete said. "She showed me the magazines."

"Suppose someone needed an Abyssinian cat with mismatched eyes," Jupiter said. "It would be easy to learn about Sphinx. As Sphinx has such a gentle nature, unlike the typical pure-bred Abyssinian, it would be easy to steal him and dye his forepaws. Now who wants Ra-Orkon very badly? Who would find it easiest to slip Sphinx into Hamid's room at night? Who knew all about the supposed curse and was trying his best to get Ra-Orkon away from the professor?"

Pete thought for a moment.

"The gardener," he said. "I mean, Achmed, Hamid's father's overseer, disguised as the gardener."

"Exactly," Jupiter said. "It would also be important to him to have the original mummy case to return the mummy in, would it not?"

"It sure would!" Pete exclaimed. "But Hamid swears that Achmed doesn't know a thing about the theft of the mummy, and had nothing to do with it."

"And Hamid believes it," Jupiter said. "But have you not noticed that an adult does not always tell all his plans to a boy, even the son of his employer? And Achmed may have some secret scheme of his own, to get hold of the mummy and then tell Hamid's father that he had to pay a very high price to obtain it. Naturally, Hamid's father would believe him. Achmed could easily get rich from such a plan."

"Whiskers!" Pete said. "He could at that. And Achmed speaks Arabic. He could make up something to sound like ancient Arabic. Hanging around outside the door, pretending to be the gardener, he could use ventriloquism to throw his voice inside and make the mummy seem to speak."

Jupiter nodded. "But," he said, "if we mention a word of our suspicions to Hamid before we can prove anything, he might tell Achmed. Achmed would then be warned and cover his traces. We must therefore divulge nothing to Hamid."

"Right," Pete said emphatically. "Now what, Jupe? We have to kill all afternoon until it's time to hear from the Ghost-to-Ghost Hookup about the marks I left on that storeroom door downtown. I suppose," he added, gloomily, "your aunt will find plenty for us to do."

"Yes, so first I'll telephone to check with Professor Yarborough and ask about Wilkins," Jupiter suggested. He dialed, and in a moment was chatting with the Egyptologist.

"Wilkins is back from the hospital," reported the professor. "He was suffering merely from shock. He said he saw the most astounding thing last night. The god Annubis, a man with a head like a jackal, appeared out of the bushes and shouted harsh words at him in a strange language. Wilkins fainted from terror. Annubis then stole Ra-Orkon."

Pete and Jupiter looked at each other.

"But we know two thieves named Joe and Harry stole Ra-Orkon," Pete said, puzzled.

"Professor," Jupiter said into the phone, "we feel sure that Wilkins was scared by someone who probably wore a rubber mask made to look like a jackal. Someone disguised as Annubis."

He then went on to relate what had happened to Pete the night before, skipping over all but the highlights.

"Yes, of course," Professor Yarborough said presently. "That would explain it. Tell me, do you think you can find the mummy case again, and do you have any idea what on earth is behind all this? Do you think that fellow Achmed is the guilty one?"

"I have a few ideas, sir," Jupiter told him. "But no proof as yet. As for the mummy case, we will hunt for that this evening. We will contact you as soon as we know anything."

He hung up and looked off into space. Pete began to fidget. "Well?" he asked. "What are you thinking now?"

"I was just thinking," Jupiter said, "that yesterday Professor Yarborough told us Wilkins had been an actor in vaudeville before he became a butler."

"Well, what about it?"

"An actor could easily pretend to be in a deep faint," Jupiter said. "Also, just suppose Wilkins' act in vaudeville was a ventriloquist act?"

"Well, was it?"

"I don't know. But suppose it was. What would that suggest?"

"Gosh!" Pete exclaimed in excitement. "That would mean that Wilkins could be guilty after all. Or he could be working with Achmed. Or he could be working with someone else altogether. Which do you think, Jupe?"

"Time," Jupiter said wisely, "will tell." And to Pete's fury, he would not speak another word about the case all afternoon.

Chapter 14

Too Many Question Marks

EARLY THAT EVENING the small salvage yard truck, with Konrad at the wheel, was bumping through the streets of downtown Los Angeles, by special permission of Mrs. Jones. Jupiter had decided that the best plan was to locate the mummy case, then hide until they saw Harry and Joe take it out of the warehouse. Then they would follow the two men and catch them in the act of turning the case over to their customer, the master thief who was apparently behind the whole mystery. Only in that way, Jupiter said, could they have positive proof.

For such a job, the gold-plated Rolls Royce would be too conspicuous. It would be spotted instantly. But the old salvage yard truck would never be noticed.

Hamid had returned to the salvage yard by taxi earlier. Now, he and Jupiter were riding in front with Konrad, and Pete and Bob were sitting on some canvas tarpaulins in the back, as the truck moved slowly through a run-down district of warehouses and small, dingy shops. During the whole trip, Bob and Pete had been arguing about whether Achmed or Wilkins would turn out to be the guilty one, and they had both changed their minds at least twice.

Now the truck pulled to a stop. Pete and Bob looked over the side. They were in front of an old, closed theater. A broken sign indicated that it was once the CHAMELOT THEATER, and on other signs there were the words: *Closed. No Trespassing. Keep out.*

Seeing Jupiter and Hamid emerge from the truck, Pete and Bob jumped down to follow them, Bob favoring his leg a bit.

"Does this look like the building you were in last night, Pete?" Jupiter asked, scowling at the crumbling old theater.

"I didn't see the front, but the building we were in wasn't that high," Pete scowled.

"Does not seem same." Hamid shook his head.

"Nevertheless, this is the address our 'ghost' gave us." Jupiter studied a slip of paper in his hand. An hour earlier, one of their 'ghosts'—one of the boys in the Ghost-to-Ghost Hookup—had phoned to say his dad had seen blue chalked question marks on a door at the rear of 10853 Chamelot Street. They had started immediately and this was certainly 10853 Chamelot Street.

"Let us look at the rear," Jupiter suggested, and led them down an alley around the building. At the rear they came out into an open space and saw, indeed, a large storeroom overhead door with several question marks chalked in blue down at one corner.

"There's your mark, Second," Jupiter said. "This must be the right place."

"It looks all wrong to me," Pete said, puzzled. "What about you, Hamid?"

"I do not think this is right," the Libyan boy said. "But it was dark. Perhaps we did not see well."

"You were in a big hurry," Jupiter said. "Look, there's a small, man-door beside the big truck door. In fact, it is open an inch. Perhaps we can peep in and spot the mummy case."

They approached the slightly open door and stooped, at various heights, to peek in. Suddenly the door was snatched open and three grinning faces appeared behind it.

"Look at Jupiter McSherlock and his stooges!" It was Skinny Norris, who laughed loudly as he spoke the words.

"Hunting for clues, Sherlock?" one of the other boys, a close crony of Skinny's, sneered.

"If it's question marks you want, just look around," the third boy, fat and red-headed, smirked. "The town's full of them."

"I guess we don't need to hang around this place any more," Skinny Norris said. "Sherlock and his men have the situation well in hand."

Snickering, they strolled past the four boys. A few steps down the alley, they all climbed into Skinny

Norris's blue sports car and drove off quickly.

It was Bob who realized first the meaning of Skinny's remark.

"Look!" he pointed to other doors backing on the alley. They all had question marks chalked on them, as far as the boys could see. "Probably all the other alleys around here are the same," he said. "All chalked up with false marks."

Jupiter's face was pink with anger.

"Skinny Norris!" he exclaimed. "One of our ghosts this morning must have telphoned him and he learned we were looking for chalked question marks. So he and his friends came down here and put question marks on this door and a lot of others just to confuse us. Then one of them telephoned us and they waited for us to arrive so they could have the laugh on us."

"They've confused us, all right," Pete growled. "And they're laughing their fool heads off. They've probably put blue question marks all over this part of town. It's a trick only Skinny would think of. When I get my hands on him I'll hammer him down to the size of a tent peg!"

Skinny Norris's malicious trick certainly seemed to have ruined any possibility of their finding the right door now. There were just too many question marks around.

"Well, what do we do now?" Bob asked helplessly. "Go back to the salvage yard?"

"Certainly not!" Jupiter snapped. "First we'll see

how many question marks Skinny and his friends scattered around. And then we'll decide on our next move. And in the future we'll have to remember that the Ghost-to-Ghost Hookup, like so many good ideas, seems to have certain weaknesses."

They spread out, searching nearby streets and alleys, after explaining swiftly to Hamid that Skinny Norris was a rival who would go to any lengths to mess up one of their investigations.

They found question marks scattered here and there for several blocks. Deeply dejected, they gathered back at the truck for further consultation.

"We'll drive around," Jupiter said doggedly. "Maybe Pete or Hamid will notice some landmark they remember from last night. We can't give up now. It's our last chance. If Harry and Joe deliver that mummy case unseen, we're licked."

With heavy hearts they climbed into the truck and Konrad began to drive slowly down Chamelot Street.

"We're beat," Pete said gloomily. "Why don't we admit it?"

"And let Skinny have the laugh on us?" Jupiter's lips set. "We'll keep trying. Now that old church on the corner—did you perhaps notice that last night while you were running?"

Pete looked at the old Spanish-mission-style church and shook his head.

"I don't think we were even on this street," he said. "The streets we were on were narrower and dingier.

And darker."

"Then we'll try another. Turn right, Konrad, please."

"Hokay," the big Bavarian said obligingly and turned right. They had gone hardly three blocks when Pete grabbed Jupiter's arm.

"That ice cream stand!" he said. "I think we went past it last night soon after we started running."

He pointed to a structure built to look like an enormous ice cream cone. It was shut and falling apart—this was a poor part of town for business.

"Stop, Konrad, please," Jupiter requested. Agreeably, Konrad stopped the truck. Pete, Jupiter, Bob, and Hamid descended and all four boys stood on the pavement, studying the cone-shaped building across the street.

"Hamid, do you remember seeing that last night?" Pete asked.

"Oh, yes," the Libyan boy nodded. "I think at the time it is some small temple. So strange among other buildings."

Bob grinned. "Here in California we have orange juice stands shaped like oranges, and hot dog stands shaped like hot dogs," he said. "A building shaped like an ice cream cone is practically normal."

"Hot dogs?" Hamid asked, horrified. "You eat dogs in America?"

But there was no time now to explain about the mysteries of the American hot dog. With a few rapid questions, Jupiter discovered that neither Pete nor

Hamid could remember which way they were running when they passed the ice cream cone building. He made a speedy decision.

"Bob, you and Hamid stay here," he said. "Keep your walkie-talkie turned on in case of further developments. Pete, you go up the street and look into all alleys to see if you recognize the right one. I will go down the street and investigate all alleys in that direction. If we find the right one, the secret symbols may still lead us to our destination. After all, Skinny and his friends couldn't cover all Los Angeles with chalk marks."

"Well, we can try it," Pete agreed.

"Konrad will stay parked here, and we will both return to this spot as our base of operations. We'll keep in touch by walkie-talkie as we hunt."

It was already twilight. Soon it would be dark. Pete and Jupiter set out in opposite directions along the street. In the truck, Hamid and Bob waited.

"Perhaps they will not find mummy case," Hamid said. "Perhaps mummy of Ra-Orkon is lost forever. Achmed and I will feel very ashamed to tell my father we lost our honored ancestor."

In spite of what Jupiter had said, Bob could see that Hamid clung to the idea that Ra-Orkon was an ancestor.

"Where is Achmed tonight?" he asked.

"I do not know," Hamid told him. "He said he had business to do for my father. He is visiting rug dealers while here, to tell them of the wares of the House of Hamid."

To Bob it sounded more as if Achmed was planning to meet the two thieves, Harry and Joe, someplace to take possession of the mummy case. But he didn't say anything to Hamid. The Libyan boy was gloomy enough.

While they talked, Pete and Jupiter had covered several blocks, looking into the alleys that usually intersected the middle of a block. By walkie-talkie they reported mutual lack of success. It was now almost too dark to see any chalk marks. With a heavy heart, Jupiter issued a command over the walkie-talkie.

"Check one more alley on your side, Second," he said. "Then rejoin me at the truck and we will discuss further strategy."

"Heard and understood," Pete's voice came back through the tiny receiver. "Out."

Jupiter plodded down the next alley. It looked much like all the others, with the backs of shops lining it, where trucks made deliveries. At the far end he could see a large building, and he headed for it. The building had a big door in the rear, but a truck stood in front of the door, a nondescript blue truck, and as Jupiter approached it, a man raised the big door so that if it had any chalk marks left by Pete—which it probably hadn't—they would not have been visible.

Jupiter stopped. He sighed. He turned to retrace his steps.

Then he stopped again. His alert ears had heard a voice.

"Okay, drive her in, Harry," one man's voice said.

"Right, Joe, stand to one side," replied the other.

Harry! Joe! The names of the two men who had carried off the mummy case!

Chapter 15

Jupiter is on His Own

JUPITER WHIRLED AND RAN toward the truck, which was easing into a dark space through the big overhead door.

There was only one chance to avoid being seen. He darted to the right side of the truck, on the side opposite Joe, who had thrust up the door. As the truck entered, he went into the dark space with it, squeezing through a two-foot space between the truck and the door frame.

Then he was inside. The truck stopped. He stopped beside it.

"I'll close the door," sang out Joe's voice. "Then you turn on the headlights, so we can see."

Crouched beside the truck, Jupiter thought swiftly. He couldn't see a thing. If he waited for the lights to come on, the men might see him. There was only one place to go where he could hope to stay undetected.

He dropped to his knees, stretched out flat on his stomach and wriggled under the truck. The noise of the closing door hid the slight sound he made. A moment later the headlights went on, illuminating the interior of the storeroom. Lying beneath the truck, Jupiter's range of vision was limited, but he could see the wheels of an antique car and beyond it what must be the mummy case of Ra-Orkon, a bulge beneath a canvas tarpaulin.

He had found the right spot. But he could not summon help because if he spoke into the walkie-talkie, which needed a firm, loud tone to operate, the men would hear him and nab him.

He waited. His heart was beating fast.

Now the driver, Harry, got out of the truck. Jupiter could see the legs of the two men only six feet from him as they stood beside the truck.

"So the customer came through, huh?" Harry chuckled. "I knew he would. He was mighty anxious to get that mummy case. What he wants with it I'll never know."

"He came through all right," his companion answered. "But get this. We're to deliver it to some other place—out beyond Hollywood. It's an empty garage, he says, and we can drive right in."

"That's all right with me."

"That's only part of it. He's afraid we might be followed. We're to take every precaution and if we think we're being followed, we don't make delivery."

"Who'd follow us?" the questioner's voice was sharp. "Nobody knows about this setup we have. We'll make delivery. I want that money he owes us."

"Sure, sure. But I haven't finished. Halfway there, if we're sure we haven't been followed, we're to stop and telephone. He might want delivery at the original address, he said. It depends."

"Depends on what?"

"He didn't say. But you haven't heard the craziest part of the whole thing yet."

"Go on, I'm listening."

"After we make delivery, he'll put the mummy back in the case. Then he wants us to take the whole thing and burn it someplace so there isn't a trace left. For that he'll pay us a thousand extra."

"A thousand extra! Why did he want us to steal the thing in the first place, if all he wants to do is burn it up?"

"Search me. Maybe he's scared and wants to get rid of the evidence. We're getting our money, so we can afford to play dumb. Let's just do as he says. Come on, let's load the case. Then we'll head out toward Hollywood."

The two pairs of legs moved away. In the light from the headlights, Jupiter saw the two men approach the mummy case and bend over it.

"Hey, we'd better check if there's anything in it," the short man, Joe, said, "Might be something valuable this customer is after."

They, lifted the lid and peered in. Joe ran his hands around the empty interior.

"Naw," he said. "Nothing. Come on, let's get it on the truck."

They pushed the mummy case to the dark space at the rear of the truck. Then they found the truck was too close to the door for them to be able to maneuver the case into it.

"Have to pull the truck forward a little," Joe said.

"You do it. I want to go get a drink of water."

Joe got into the truck, the motor roared, and the truck moved forward several feet. As it moved, it left Jupiter behind so that he was no longer beneath it. Harry disappeared through a small door.

Jupiter was faced with a tough dilemma. If he tried to call Pete and the others on the walkie-talkie, he'd be heard. If he crawled into a corner and hid behind some barrels he saw, the truck would get away and he wouldn't be able to follow it. If he climbed into the truck itself, the men would see him when they put the mummy case in.

For a frantic moment he could see no way to hide and at the same time keep track of the truck and the mummy case until he could contact the others to follow it to its destination.

Then, in a burst of inspiration, he saw how he could manage it.

Harry was still in the washroom. Joe was still behind the wheel. Unseen, Jupiter crawled to the mummy case lying on the concrete floor. He lifted the lid, wriggled inside like a plump eel, and eased the lid back down,

being careful to hold the end of the lid up with a pencil, just enough to give him air.

Then, with his heart in his throat, he waited.

Back at the salvage yard truck Pete, Bob, and Hamid
were gathered on the pavement. They were worried.
Some time had passed since the last order had come
from Jupiter, and since then only silence had answered
their efforts to reach him by walkie-talkie. Had he gotten himself into some kind of serious trouble?

Then words crackled into Pete's receiver.

"First Investigator calling Second Investigator. Are
you reading me, Second?"

"Second Investigator calling. Affirmative. Affirmative. I am reading you, First. What's happened?"

"The truck we want is heading for Hollywood,"
came Jupiter's voice. "It's a blue, two-ton truck with
some peeling paint. The license number is PX 1043.
At this moment it is heading west on Painter Street.
Have you got that?"

"Affirmative!" Pete yelled. Jupiter's message meant
that the truck was on the same street they were, heading away from them. It could only be a few blocks
away, Jupiter's voice was coming in so strongly.

"We'll turn around and follow it right away, First!"
Pete added. "Where are you?"

"I am where you were last night," Jupiter replied.

"Inside the mummy case?" Pete yelled.

"Strapped in, unfortunately," Jupiter answered. "It

was the only way I could maintain contact. Please do not lose sight of the truck. I will need help when we contact the man who is to receive the case."

"We'll stay right behind you," Pete said, and swiftly the group swung into action. The three boys clambered into the truck. Pete told Konrad what to do. The big Bavarian turned the truck around. He gunned the motor and the salvage yard truck covered several blocks swiftly. Soon it came up behind a shabby blue truck with the license number Jupiter had given them. Then Konrad dropped back half a block and kept at that distance.

The big street lights on the boulevard they now entered fortunately provided enough illumination for them all to see the blue truck at a considerable distance.

"We're half a block behind you now, First," Pete said into his walkie-talkie. "Have you any idea where you're headed for?"

"Negative," Jupiter's voice answered. "Joe received a destination over the phone from his customer."

"Is like a movie!" Hamid said excitedly. "Only more exciting. But I worry about First Investigator Jupiter if we lose the truck and are not there to help when he is discovered."

"So do we, Hamid," Bob muttered.

For that matter, Jupiter was worrying, too. Stretched out inside the mummy case, keeping his nose close to the crack that admitted air, he was wondering if he had done the right thing. But hiding inside the evidence was the only way he could possibly keep track of the mummy case.

Still, things seemed to be going along smoothly. Now they had covered several miles, and Konrad and the others were still behind the blue truck. Harry and Joe hadn't noticed anything apparently. Jupiter was beginning to relax and congratulate himself when the truck suddenly speeded up. It bounced roughly, as if crossing railroad tracks. Behind them came a clang-clang of crossing bells, and the hoot of a Diesel train horn. A roaring noise of a train rushed by behind them, hardly twenty feet away.

Then into Jupiter's receiver came a frantic call from Pete.

"First! We're blocked by a freight train. It looks about a mile long. By the time it passes, we'll have lost you. Can you read me?"

"Affirmative!" Jupiter yelled. He gulped, then, as he was trying to think what to suggest, the truck made a sharp turn and started in a new direction.

"Second!" Jupe said sharply. "Truck has changed direction. I do not know what street we are on now. But I have a suggestion. Can you still read me?"

"First!" Pete's voice had become faint and indistinct. "I can't understand what you're saying. You just faded out on me. Can you——"

Then Pete's voice died out in static. Jupiter knew they were now beyond communication range of the small walkie-talkies. There was practically no chance at all that Konrad would be able to locate the blue truck again.

He was on his own!

Chapter 16

Captive and Captor

FOR SEVERAL MINUTES Jupiter waited, hoping to hear Pete's voice come in over his walkie-talkie. But it didn't. Obviously, by the time the train had passed, they had hopelessly lost the truck. He could imagine Konrad speeding up and down sidestreets, looking for a trace of the blue truck they had been following. But in the darkness, and with Los Angeles' confusing streets, there wasn't one chance in a million of their finding it.

He tried sending out a message of his own.

"Hello, Second Investigator," he said. "This is First Investigator calling. Can you read me? Can you read me?"

He got no answer from Pete. He did get an answer from an unknown voice that sounded like a boy his own age.

"Hello," it said. "Who's talking? What's this Second Investigator and First Investigator stuff? Are you playing some kind of game? If you are, let me in on it."

"Listen," Jupiter spoke swiftly. "I'm not playing any game. Will you call the police for me?"

"Call the police? What for?" the boy's voice asked.

Jupiter thought swiftly. The whole truth would sound too hard to believe.

"I'm locked in the back of a truck," he said. "The men driving it don't know I'm here. I want to get out. Call the police. Have them stop the truck and let me out."

He had decided that it was time for outside help. And only the police could locate the truck and rescue him in time.

"Sure, I'll do that," the boy replied. "Hitching a ride, huh, and you got locked in? Say, better talk fast, you were starting to fade just now."

"I'll talk fast," Jupiter exclaimed. "Listen, it's a blue, two-ton truck with license plates PX 1043. It's heading for Hollywood and should be going through Hollywood in about ten minutes. It's old and beat up and—"

But the other boy's voice cut him off.

"What's wrong?" the boy asked. "I just heard a couple of words and you faded out. You must be moving away from me. Can you read me?"

"I can read you," Jupiter said. "Can you still read me?"

"Hello! Hello!" the boy cried. "I can't get you at all. You must have moved out of transmitting range for your set. Sorry."

Disheartened, Jupiter wondered what to do now. He slipped the walkie-talkie back inside his shirt and tried to think of some plan of action. For once, nothing helpful occurred to him. Harry and Joe had strapped the case shut before hoisting it into the truck. So he couldn't get out.

But he wasn't worried about that. Enough air came in the crack for him to breathe. What worried him was what lay ahead. He swallowed hard as he pictured the scene when the truck would come to a stop, when Harry and Joe would take the mummy case out, unstrap it—and open it.

And there would be Jupiter Jones, like an oyster when its shell is opened: And just about as helpless.

Thinking about that, Jupiter broke into a sweat. Harry and Joe and the customer would all be gathered around the mummy case, looking down into it, and there he would be, looking up at them. They would be three dangerous criminals and he would be a witness, someone who could send them to jail.

Jupiter tried not to think of what dangerous criminals did to potential witnesses if they could. Instead, he tried to think of some positive line of action. Suppose the instant the lid was lifted, he leaped out and started to run? That might take them by surprise. He might break free and get away from them.

But he gloomily doubted it. There would be three of them. No matter which way he jumped one of them would be close enough to grab him. He wondered if his aunt and uncle would miss him. And Pete and Bob—suppose they never knew what became of him? Suppose they had to spend the rest of their lives wondering what had happened to him.

The thought brought a large lump into his throat. Then suddenly the truck stopped. Jupiter tensed, thinking that the moment had come. But nothing seemed to happen and in five minutes the truck started up again. Then he remembered that Joe had said they were to call the customer before making delivery. Probably they had been making the phone call during the stop. What the result was, he had no idea.

As the truck rolled on, his gloomy thoughts had a chance to get started again. He was making a number of good resolutions about what he would do next time —if there ever was a next time—when abruptly he became alert. The truck had stopped once more. He heard a noise, like the sound of a garage door being rolled up. He knew they had arrived, and at once he tensed for action. His gloom vanished. He wasn't going to just lie there helplessly when the case was opened. Suppose there were three of them? He'd bowl over the smallest one and run for it. He'd fight to the last!

The truck doors were opening now. By ear he followed the events outside. That scrambling sound was Joe and Harry climbing into the back of the truck. Yes, now they were lifting the mummy case. One of them almost dropped it.

"There's something pretty peculiar about this

mummy case," Joe said. "Back in the storeroom, when we pushed it, it didn't seem this heavy. Then when we picked it up to put it in the truck, it felt a lot heavier. Now it's still heavy."

Another time, Jupiter would have grinned. It was easy to imagine Joe's puzzlement. After all, he had slipped into the case back in the warehouse before they lifted it onto the truck, adding well over a hundred pounds to its weight. Naturally the changing weight baffled them. But Jupiter couldn't grin. Not now.

He braced himself as the wooden mummy case was half lifted and half slid out of the truck to the ground. Then he heard another voice.

"Bring it inside the garage, quickly!" The voice was too muffled to identify. But the mummy case was lifted and carried, then set down with a plop on a cement floor.

"All right," said the third voice. "Leave me alone with it for ten minutes, then you can take the case and the mummy away and burn them."

"First we want our money." That was Joe. "Before we leave you alone with it. Our money or we take it away again."

"All right, all right, I have it in my pocket. Two thousand dollars. Get that door shut and I'll pay you outside—half now and half when you take it away and burn it."

"Let me get my strap off before I forget it." That was Harry. "I'll need it again."

The case rocked as the strap was loosened. Then Joe spoke.

"Leave it, stupid!" he said. "We'll need it when we take the case away again."

"Okay, okay," Harry grumbled. "I'll put it back on later. Let's get our money first."

"Come on outside and I'll pay you." The unknown "customer" sounded nervous, as if anxious to get them away from the mummy case and outside as fast as possible.

Jupiter heard the sound of a garage door sliding down. This was followed by silence. Cautiously he pushed up the lid. He peeped out. He was in a dark garage, but he could see he was alone. Swiftly he pushed the lid up and clambered out. He put the lid back in place and looked around for the ordinary door that should be there, for entrance when not driving a car into the garage. He located it by a light outside shining through its glass pane, and started toward it. At that moment the door began to open and Jupiter flattened himself against the wall of the garage. The opening door hid him.

The dim figure of the man who entered closed the door and then, to Jupiter's dismay, locked it tightly with a key. But he did not see the figure of the boy crouching in the corner. Instead he turned toward the mummy case on the garage floor, rubbing his hands gloatingly.

"At last I have you," he said out loud. "After

all these years. Twenty-five years I've waited. But it's worth it, it's worth every minute of it."

He took a flashlight from his pocket and played it on the lid of the mummy case. Apparently he wanted to be quite alone, and did not turn on the garage lights lest Joe and Harry, outside, might peer in to see what he was doing.

After studying the case, he lifted the lid off and laid it on the floor. He bent over to run his hands along the inside of the case as if feeling for something.

And Jupiter acted on impulse.

He took three steps toward the man and pushed.

The dark figure, already bent far into the mummy case, gave a strangled cry and toppled completely into it, except for his feet. Jupiter pushed the feet so the man was totally inside the mummy case. With the speed of desperation, he lifted the lid and covered the case.

He had the "customer," the master thief who had engineered the theft of the mummy and the case, trapped inside the mummy case itself!

But could he keep him there?

Jupiter sat on the lid, hard and swiftly, before the startled man inside could attempt to lift it. Under him the lid tilted and rocked as his prisoner fought to get out, but Jupiter's weight was far too much to unseat uneasily. Jupiter held on, the sweat pouring from his face, intent on keeping the lid down.

The man inside beat on the lid with his fists and

tried to shout as he struggled to get out.

"Joe! Harry! What do you think you're doing?"

The words were only a muffled murmur. Without something to hold one end up a little, the lid was a tight fit. Joe and Harry, outside, could not hear.

But in a moment, Jupiter knew, they would get impatient and would investigate. They would find him. Then what would happen to him?

Chapter 17

Amazing Revelations

ALL JUPITER COULD DO was sit where he was and keep his captive imprisoned. If Joe and Harry rolled up the big car door and saw him——

Then Jupiter heard voices outside. Shouts. Cries of alarm and dismay. A horn honked wildly. More yells. Sounds of a scuffle.

He had no time to wonder what was going on. His prisoner had turned around so that he could press upward with his back, and little by little the lid was rising. In another moment, despite all Jupiter's efforts, it would pitch to one side and fling him to the floor.

Just then, the big car door rolled up with a clang. Someone cried, "Who's in there?" Then a hand found the light switch beside the door. A bright overhead light sprang on. The man in the mummy case abruptly ceased struggling, as if aware of the interruption.

Jupiter blinked at the group who stood just outside the garage door. The group consisted of Pete and Bob and Hamid, with Professor Yarborough and Achmed.

A moment later they were joined by Konrad, who rubbed his hands with pleasure.

"Got those two tied up good with rope from truck," Konrad said. Then he caught sight of the perspiring Jupiter. "Jupe!" he called. "You hokay?"

"I'm fine." Jupe spoke almost normally, but it was an effort. "How did you all get here?"

It was Bob who answered, the others seeming too perplexed by the odd scene to speak immediately.

"When we lost you and the truck, we——" He stopped as a sudden violent movement by the man trapped inside the mummy case almost sent Jupiter tumbling. "Who've you got in there?" he asked, eyes bulging.

"Yes," Professor Yarborough now put in, blinking owlishly behind his gold-framed lenses. "Who on earth is in the mummy case?"

Jupiter mopped his face with a handkerchief.

"The man who started all this six months ago," he said. "The magician beggar, Sardon, who visited Hamid's father and convinced him that Ra-Orkon was his ancestor. Sardon, who wanted Hamid's father to make an effort to steal the mummy, so that when Sardon stole it himself, the House of Hamid would be thought guilty."

"Sardon? Sardon is here?" cried the boy Hamid. "I cannot understand."

"It is not possible!" exclaimed his guardian, the dark-complexioned Achmed. "Sardon is in Libya!"

"I'll show you," Jupiter said. "I guess we can stop him if he tries to get away."

He slipped down from the lid of the mummy case. It immediately flew off and fell to the floor. A very flushed and disheveled man rose to his feet and stared wildly at them.

"Sardon!" cried Hamid. "That is not Sardon! Sardon is blind in one eye, with long, white hair, and is very crippled, and walks with a stick."

"Disguise," Jupiter answered. "The cat of Ra-Orkon was really Mrs. Banfry's cat in disguise. The gardener was Achmed in disguise. The god Annubis was really the thief Harry in disguise. And all along Sardon has been someone in disguise, too—this man here."

"Freeman!" gasped Professor Yarborough, gazing in astonishment at the man standing in the mummy case. "What on earth does this mean? You stole Ra-Orkon? You stole the mummy case? I mean, had them stolen?"

The fight had gone out of Professor Freeman. He saw that no escape was possible.

"Yes, Yarborough," he said. "I have been waiting twenty-five years to get my hands on that mummy and its case—almost since the time it was discovered. Now, thanks to a pack of nosy boys, I have lost a million dollars. Perhaps two million."

"Yes!" It was Achmed who spoke. He stepped forward, stared hard into Professor Freeman's face. "It is Sardon! The face is the same, with brown stain removed. The voice, the same. This is the man who came

to my master's home and spun for him a fairy tale
that the mummy of Ra-Orkon was his ancestor. This is
the man who persuaded my master to send me here to
get back Ra-Orkon so that we might set his spirit at
peace. Liar!"

And he spat into Professor Freeman's face.

The language expert wiped his face with a weary
gesture.

"I guess I deserved that, and more," he said. "I'll
explain everything. Right now I suppose you want to
know why I wanted Ra-Orkon so badly."

"I certainly do," Professor Yarborough cried. "Why,
you could have come and studied him at my home all
you wanted."

"I didn't really want Ra-Orkon at all," Professor
Freeman said, stepping out of the mummy case. "I
wanted this wooden case which held him. You see, my
father was with you when you discovered Ra-Orkon,
Yarborough."

"Of course he was," the white-haired man cried. "A
very good man, too. His murder in the bazaar of Cairo
greatly distressed me."

"Well," Professor Freeman said, "my father made a
discovery you knew nothing about. Going over the
mummy case when he was alone, he found a secret
cavity in it closed by a solid plug of wood. Inside the
cavity——here, I'll show you."

From the wall he took a small saw. He turned the
mummy case on its side and was about to apply the

saw to one corner when Professor Yarborough stopped him.

"Don't!" he shouted. "You told me this was a priceless relic."

"Not as valuable as what's inside," Professor Freeman managed a wan smile. "Besides, you need a bit of the wood for your carbon dating experiment. Frankly, I'd never have had to steal the mummy case if my father hadn't glued the secret hiding place shut so tightly it has to be sawed open. Otherwise I could have opened it sometime at my leisure at your home. But my father was taking no chances. He hoped to get the mummy case for himself, somehow, someday, and he made sure no one else would discover his secret.

"You see"—Professor Freeman was sawing now, taking a large piece off one corner—"my father wrote everything out in a letter to be sent to me in case anything happened to him before he got the mummy case. The letter came to me after his death. I was a college student studying languages at the time. I immediately made the languages of the Middle East my specialty, so that in later years I could visit Egypt and try to obtain the mummy from the museum there. I couldn't manage it. But then, six months ago, Yarborough, you yourself told me the museum was going to send the mummy to you.

"I made a flying trip to Egypt, found that I could not obtain the case, and concocted a plan to persuade some rich Libyan that Ra-Orkon was his ancestor. I disguised myself as Sardon, a beggar-magician, and visited Hamid, senior, a wealthy Libyan rug-dealer. With my knowledge of languages, I had no trouble speaking in strange tongues when I pretended to be in a trance. I convinced Hamid of the House of Hamid so completely that he sent his overseer and his son here to get the mummy back for him—to steal it if necessary, which was just what I wanted.

"Of course, all along I was prepared to steal the mummy and its case myself, if I couldn't get it any other way. I wanted the House of Hamid to be blamed if that happened. I knew that whoever Hamid, senior, sent would take time to make preparations, and I was sure he would first visit you to ask for the mummy, and that you would refuse.

"In this way, if I had to steal the mummy, suspicion would be directed at the House of Hamid, not at me. I hoped, however, that it might not be necessary for me to steal it. I hoped that I could scare you by making the mummy whisper. I thought you would become so nervous that you would want to get the mummy and its case out of your house and would put it in my care to see if I could interpret the mysterious whispering. I could have worked at my leisure to open the mummy case, and then I would have given you back your precious Ra-Orkon, "cured" of its bad habit of whispering.

"But you were stubborn. Besides you said you were going to saw off a piece of the case for testing and I

was afraid you might discover what was hidden inside.
I had to work fast if I wanted to get at the case first, so
I hired professional thieves to steal it. Then—Ah! Here
we are."

The sawed corner broke free. All of them could see
a dark crevice in the solid wood of the bottom of the
mummy case.

"I thought it sounded a little hollow," Professor Yarborough murmured, as Freeman plucked at some
parchment plugging the crevice.

"I know," the other man said. "You see I had to act
quickly—before you became too curious and perhaps
investigated. Now let us see what my father discovered,
there in a dark tomb in Egypt twenty-five years ago."

He pulled out the parchment, which made a sizable
bundle. Carefully he laid it on the floor and unrolled
it. When the last wrapping was turned back, all of those
watching gasped. Liquid fire in blue and green and
orange and crimson seemed to glow on the floor of the
garage.

"Jewels," Professor Yarborough gasped. "Ancient
jewels from the days of the Pharaohs! They're worth a
fortune as jewels, and worth many times more because
of their antiquity."

"Now you understand why the mummy case meant
so much to me, and why I went to such great lengths
to secure it," Professor Freeman sighed. "My father
dared not try to carry these away with him. He took
just two or three and put the rest back for another

time. I have always felt his murder in Cairo was because of his possession of the jewels, which he probably tried to sell."

Professor Yarborough blinked.

"I begin to have a theory," he said. "About Ra-
Orkon, I mean. Where is he?"

"Over there." Professor Freeman pointed to the rear
of the garage. "He's safe under some burlap."

"Thank goodness!" breathed Professor Yarborough.
"My theory——" He stopped abruptly. "But that can
wait," he said. "You have a lot more to explain, Freeman. In the first place, how did you make the mummy
whisper to me?"

Professor Freeman's shoulders sagged. He looked
like a man who has seen his life's ambition taken from
him.

"Bring the jewels into the house," he said, "and I'll
tell you everything."

Chapter 18

Mr. Hitchcock Asks
Some Questions

THE FAMED DIRECTOR, Alfred Hitchcock, sat behind his desk in his office and put down the last sheet of paper containing the story of The Three Investigators' adventures in solving the mystery of the whispering mummy. He looked across the desk at Jupiter, Bob, and Pete as they perched on the edges of chairs.

"Well done, lads," he rumbled. "However, I can see that there were some tense moments before success came."

Tense moments? Pete, remembering his trip in the mummy case, gulped. Jupiter, however, now that it was all over, had a look of satisfaction on his round features.

"Yes, sir," he said. "Then you'll introduce the story for us?"

"I will indeed," Mr. Hitchcock told him. "First, however, there are a few small points I would like to clear up."

"Did I leave something out?" Bob, who had been

responsible for writing up all the notes, asked anxiously.

"One or two explanations," Alfred Hitchcock told him. "For which I do not blame you, as explanations make dry reading in an exciting story. However, I should like to know them."

"Yes, sir!" Bob said.

"Let me see"—Mr. Hitchcock put his finger tips together—"I believe the background of events is clear to me. Twenty-five years ago my friend, Professor Yarborough, discovered Ra-Orkon. At that time Aleph Freeman, Professor Freeman's father, discovered that the mummy case hid a fortune in jewels and determind to try to gain them for himself. He was killed before he could do so, but had passed the knowledge on to his son, who made it his life's ambition to find the jewels."

"Yes, sir." Bob put in. "Professor Yarborough has a theory now about why Ra-Orkon was buried so plainly and simply, with only his cat, in a secret tomb. There were many grave robbers in those days who opened the graves of the kings for the valuable objects inside. Ra-Orkon's relatives hoped the robbers would be fooled into thinking he wasn't worth bothering with, while all the time he had his jewel collection buried with him."

"Very plausible," said the director. "But let me continue. Professor Freeman disguised himself as the magician, Sardon, and spun a fancy story to get the House of Hamid involved in the case, planning to use them to cover his own tracks. Having seen a picture of Mrs. Banfry's cat, and recognizing its similarity to the cat of Ra-Orkon long ago, he worked that into his story to make it seem even more plausible. Later he stole Mrs. Banfry's cat, disguised it, and slipped it into Hamid's home."

"Yes, sir," Jupiter nodded. "He admitted all that."

"Thus," said Mr. Hitchcock, "Achmed and Hamid in trying to get the mummy were actually carrying out Freeman's plan. Freeman made the mummy whisper, hoping Yarborough would lend it to him. When that did not work, he hired Joe and Harry to steal it. He was very upset when they brought him only the mummy because all along it was really the mummy case he wanted."

"That's it, sir," Bob said. "They actually delivered the mummy while Jupe and the Professor and I were at Professor Freeman's house listening to the tape. Worthington would have seen them except he had to park down the road a hundred yards. That was when Professor Freeman came back with ginger ale, to cover up the reason he was absent so long. Also, that was when he sent them back after the mummy case, and kept us there a long time listening to the tape to give them the chance to steal it. It was his idea for them to use jackal masks for disguise, in case Wilkins saw them."

"He was undoubtedly clever," Alfred Hitchcock

agreed. "However, Pete, you and Hamid trailed the mummy case by the unusual method of riding in it. I quite understand how you, young Jones, found the case again. But now we come to something I do not understand."

He frowned and stared at them. They wriggled uneasily.

"Yes, sir?" Jupiter asked in an unusually meek voice.

"After the other boys lost track of you and the blue truck," the director thundered, "how did it happen they broke in just at the spot where you had trapped Professor Freeman, and just at the moment you needed them?"

"You'd better answer that, Pete," Jupiter suggested.

"Sure thing," Pete said. "I mean, yes, sir. Well you see, Mr. Hitchcock, after we lost the blue truck, we decided Achmed had to be guilty. We went straight to Professor Yarborough's house, got him, and hurried to Achmed's house. But Achmed was just saying good night to some rug buyers. He was as surprised as anybody by what we told him. Since he couldn't be guilty, we decided to call the police. But before we did that Professor Yarborough wanted some advice from his friend Professor Freeman about what to tell the police, so——"

"Do not tell me," rumbled Alfred Hitchcock. "I begin to see. You all hurried to Freeman's home. There in front of his garage was the blue truck. En route, when the men phoned him, he told them to deliver the case there as originally planned, since no one was around to interfere. Yarborough's desire for his friend's advice thereby brought you to the scene in the nick of time."

"Yes, sir," Jupiter agreed. "Harry and Joe were arrested. They have a long criminal record. The professor is trying to get Professor Freeman off, though. He says he isn't a professional criminal and will probably never do anything wrong again. Professor Freeman has resigned from the university and wants to go to the Middle East to use his knowledge of languages to work for the United Nations. Professor Yarborough is going to send the jewels back to Egypt. We restored Sphinx to Mrs. Banfry, and Hamid and Achmed have returned to Libya. They were glad to have the deception discovered in time. Hamid has promised to send us an Oriental rug especially for our Headquarters with our question-mark symbol woven into the design. So I guess that covers everything." ·

"Not quite!" Alfred Hitchcock bellowed, fixing Jupiter with a piercing stare. "You have left out the greatest mystery of the whole case. *How did the mummy whisper?*"

"Oh, that." Jupiter's round features may have hidden a smile. "Ventriloquism, sir, just as Bob's father originally suggested."

Mr. Hitchcock's expression grew sterner.

"Young man, I have been in show business for many years. I know quite well that ventriloquists do *not* throw their voices, as is generally believed. They create an illusion of a dummy talking, but to do so they must be close to it. They cannot cast their voices from a distance!"

Bob and Pete glanced at each other. They had always believed ventriloquists could cast their voices. Jupiter merely nodded.

"Yes, sir," he said. "But Professor Freeman could. You see, sir, he was always so far away from the scene that at first I did not suspect him. I should have, because after all, he knew many Eastern languages and if anyone could make a mummy seem to whisper ancient Arabic, it was Professor Freeman.

"But I didn't suspect him until I found that the cat had been disguised, which made me think the whole story of Sardon had something peculiar about it. Then I began to wonder if Sardon was a real beggar or someone in disguise. If he was someone in disguise, he had to be Professor Freeman because his father, who had worked with Yarborough, knew about the mummy and Freeman was the only person in the whole case who could have talked fluently to Mr. Hamid, and then spoken in strange languages in a pretended trance."

"Well reasoned." The director nodded. "But you haven't answered my question."

"No, sir, but I'm coming to it." Jupiter told him. "As a speech expert, Professor Freeman was accustomed to using different kinds of microphones and recording devices. I'm sure you know, sir, that there is in use now

a special parabolic microphone which can pick up a
conversation from hundreds of feet away when prop-
erly focused?"

Enlightenment spread across Alfred Hitchcock's face.

"Of course," he said. "Go on, young Jones,"

"Well, sir, there are also directional speakers that
can focus a voice in a tight line and project it for hundreds of feet, so that it can be heard only in one spot.
Professor Freeman had a speaker like that on his bal-
cony. His home is on the side of a canyon directly
across from Professor Yarborough's, about three hundred feet away.

"So Professor Freeman made a tape of something
that sounded like ancient Arabic. Using a telescope,
when he saw his friend Professor Yarborough working
in the museum room with the big windows open—and
Professor Yarborough hates closed windows—he only
had to turn on the tape recorder and project the message across the valley, to a spot where it could be heard
only when one was very close to the mummy.

"He usually did it afternoons when he was back
from his work, and he did it only when Professor Yarborough was alone in the room—except for the time
when I disguised myself as the professor. That was how
the mummy seemed to recognize Professor Yarborough,
sir, and wouldn't talk for anybody else.

"When Professor Freeman agreed to drive over to
examine the mummy, he put the tape on before he left
his home. The tape was timed so that there would be a
few moments of silence, then the strange sound would

start again while he was on his way and stop by the time he reached Professor Yarborough's house. He wanted to be sure to avoid suspicion.

"The night Harry and Joe put on jackal masks and stole the mummy, Professor Freeman took enough time to slip upstairs and talk into the speaker, aiming it at Wilkins. He knew this would frighten the old gentleman into a faint. So you see, it really was a kind of voice-casting or ventriloquism—you could call it scientific ventriloquism."

"Amazing," Alfred Hitchcock said slowly. "So Sphinx is restored to Mrs. Banfry, the mummy has stopped whispering, the jewels will go back to Egypt, and the case is solved. I can't help wondering what adventure you lads will get into next."

"Well, sir," Bob said, taking a piece of paper from his pocket, "we have several possibilities. There's ____"

"No!" The director held up his hand. "Don't tell me. I might find myself wondering about them when I should be doing more important things. Let it come as a surprise to me. Now good day, boys, I really have work to do."

As the boys filed out, the man behind the desk glanced at the sheaf of papers they had left with him. In spite of his words he couldn't help wondering what adventure The Three Investigators would find themselves in next. Whatever it was, it would be something unusual.

Of that he had no doubt.